In the Halls of the Haunted

Jay D Falor

Misfit Fantasy
Published by Misfit Pages
Texas USA

On the World Wide Web at
www.misfitpages.com

First Published 2025

ISBN: 978-1-962613-22-4
(First edition)

DEDICATION

To my family, whose stories and support have fueled my imagination. And to my brother, who at four years old met the "pretty lady" who visited him one night and gave us all chills—thank you for making ghosts feel so real.

CONTENTS

ACKNOWLEDGMENTS

To my family, who has always supported my love of ghost
stories and mysteries, and to my editor, Amy, whose
guidance brought this book to life—thank you.

1

Wesley pulled up to the Hawthorne Estate, his car laden with grocery bags filled with fresh produce, cold cuts and a few other things. The late afternoon sun cast long shadows across the house which loomed before him, its Victorian grandeur both inviting and slightly intimidating. He stepped out of the car, the crunch of gravel under his feet interrupted by the loud ringtone of his phone.

"Hey Charlie," Wesley answered, juggling the collection of grocery bags he'd accumulated from his trip.

"Hey Wes, how's the new house?"

"I had no idea how much I hated paperwork until we were finishing up closing on this house, I swear."

Charlie laughed. "You live for paperwork, man. What are you talking about?"

Wesley balanced the phone between his shoulder and ear as he closed and locked the car doors. "That's different and you know it."

"I wouldn't be able to stand all the research write ups you've done."

Wesley snorted. "True. House paperwork still sucks, though, even if it was necessary."

"So, how's the moving going?"

"Movers just finished this afternoon. You caught me coming back from the store."

The were sounds of a slight scuffle from Charlie's side of the call as Wesley opened the front door, shouldering his way inside.

"Daddy, who is it?"

"It's Wes, Teddy."

Wesley heard the kid let out a cheer.

"Uncle Wes!" It seemed like Charlie must have put the phone on speaker, since Teddy's voice rang through loud and clear.

"Hey kiddo. You excited?"

As Wesley entered the foyer, the heavy wooden door creaked shut behind him, sealing him in the cool, dim interior. He hefted his groceries over to one arm to flip on the lights as Teddy regaled him with everything he could think of.

"...And I'm bringing Mr Lion, 'cause he needs to see your new house too," Teddy told him seriously.

"I can't wait to meet him," he replied.

The grand staircase stretched upwards, its ornate banister

disappearing into the shadows of the upper floor. Wesley set the grocery bags down on the original oak flooring for a second to rest his arm and fingers, the sound reverberating through the still somewhat empty foyer. He couldn't shake the feeling of being watched, as if the house itself was observing him, waiting to see what he would do next. It was possible that the long trip here had decided to mess with him since he'd skipped that last rest-stop on the drive over. He shook off that thought, focusing instead on Teddy.

"I found your juice, and those fudge toaster pastries will be waiting for you when you get here, Ted." Wesley gave his arm a good shake to rid the pins and needles before collecting his grocery bags and heading for the kitchen.

There was another scuffle at the other end, Teddy's shouting of 'He got them, daddy!' growing fainter. Wesley sighed; hopefully the kid would grow out of leaving the room mid-call like that sometime soon. In the meantime he'd switch to speaker himself and begin unpacking his haul and properly stocking his fridge. He figured it would be a while.

"So, toaster pastries?"

Wesley swore, almost dropping the jar of pasta sauce he'd been about to set down in the fridge door. He heard Charlie attempting to stifle his laughter.

"You haven't been that colorful in ages, man."

"Yes, and I found that one brand of pizza rolls you like."

"Don't side-step the - Shit, seriously? You found those? I can't seem to find them here at all, you legend!"

"I got all the classics here waiting for you two," Wesley

smiled, dropping an assortment of carrots, squash and spinach in the vegetable drawer. "We're going to have a guy's night of junk food, before I go back to eating healthy after all the take-out I've had on the move down here."

"Guy's night?" Teddy piped up from somewhere in the background.

"Yeah kiddo; all three of us. It'll be fun."

"No," Charlie said a moment later, somewhat muffled. "You don't put those in there. They go in the other case."

"Why?"

"Because it makes things easier, Teddy." He heard Charlie reply. "I promise."

Wesley snorted. "Got help, huh?"

Charlie sighed dramatically. "The joys of raising a four year old. You sure you don't want in on this?"

"Nope. That's all yours, my friend." As he placed the last of the perishables in the fridge, he heard a soft thud from upstairs.

"Suit yourself, man-."

 "Hang on," Wesley froze, listening. Silence.

"Everything alright, Wes?" Charlie tone shifted from amusement to mild concern.

He shrugged it off. "Could have sworn I heard something, but I bet it's the old house settling."

 "If you say so, man." Charlie replied.

But as he turned to put away the grocery bags, Wesley heard it again. This time, there was no mistaking it. Something was upstairs.

"Shit."

"I hope we can keep the swearing down a bit more after Teddy and I arrive. I'm trying to keep him from picking up bad habits. Felicia would kill me if Teddy started repeating us."

Wesley sighed, switching his phone back from speaker mode as he made his way to the grand staircase. He collected a mop by the railing that he hadn't put away yet, just in case.

"I get that, Charlie; your mother-in-law is a formidable woman." He placed his foot on the first step, the wood creaking under his weight. He paused again, listening. More silence.

"Great; probably a squirrel or a raccoon somehow made it inside."

"Aren't they supposed to make sure that's all clear before signing off?"

"Yeah, the inspector likely missed a spot in their run-over for the house." He took a deep breath and began to climb, adjusting his grip on the mop.

The thud sounded again, louder.

"Whoa, okay, I heard that this time," Charlie said.

"Hopefully I don't have to call animal control," Wesley remarked as he reached the top of the stairs and turned towards the master bedroom. It was at that moment the phone call cut off.

* * *

Wesley's phone rang again, the sudden noise slicing through the silence like a knife. He answered quickly. "Charlie?"

"Yeah, man. Call got dropped. Everything all right?" Charlie's voice was laced with concern.

"Yeah," Wesley replied. "It's weird. I got good reception; it shouldn't have cut off like that."

He pushed open the master bedroom door, the mop clutched tightly in his hand. The room was bathed in the fading light of the setting sun, casting long, dancing shadows across the hardwood floor. "I'm just checking the bedroom now."

"Be careful, Uncle Wes!" Teddy's voice piped up from the background.

Wesley smiled. "I will, kiddo." He stepped into the room, his eyes scanning the clutter of moving boxes and newly assembled furniture. The thudding sound had seemed to come from in here, but now, everything was still.

He moved cautiously, his senses on high alert. The room smelled of dust and old wood, a testament to the house's age and probably a warning that it needed another good vacuum and dusting. The boxes were stacked haphazardly, some open, their contents peeking out like half-told secrets. He frowned, a niggle of unease burrowing deeper. He was sure he hadn't left them like that.

"Anything?" Charlie asked, his voice barely above a

whisper.

"Not yet," Wesley murmured, reaching out with the mop to tap a few of the boxes before jumping back, in case something furry scurried out at him, but nothing moved. No scurrying of tiny feet, no rustle of disturbed packaging. Just the stillness and the dust motes dancing in the sunlight.

He tapped a few more boxes in the same manner, the frown deepening on his face. Nothing. No sign of any critter, no hint of what could have caused the noise. Just the open boxes, their contents seemingly undisturbed.

"Wes?" Charlie's voice was a quiet prompt in his ear.

Wesley let out a sigh, leaning on the mop and running a hand through his hair. "I don't see anything, Charlie. Just some open boxes, but nothing seems to be missing. Though I don't remember opening any of these boxes just yet."

There was a pause on the other end of the line. Then, Charlie asked, "Think it could've been something falling over?"

Wesley looked around the room, his eyes lingering on the open boxes. "Maybe," he said, but there was this odd feeling he couldn't quite shake off. He'd been in this room later that morning, after the movers had finished bringing in his bed frame, dresser and bedside table. None of the boxes lined against the wainscoting had been opened then, either.

"I think I have to call the moving company. I hope someone didn't try to open the boxes to try to help unpack, but I can't be too sure."

"They usually send a good crew," Charlie replied. "You taking photos?"

"Yup." Wesley put the phone back on speaker to switch to the camera app. "On it now." Though nothing looked out of place as he checked each opened box further; all of his knick-knacks were still wrapped in old newspaper and his framed pictures were untouched.

"I was planning to do a sweep of the house either this evening or tomorrow, in case they'd left any of their equipment behind, but I guess I have more to look out for."

Something was off. Wesley just couldn't put his finger on what it was.

* * *

Wesley woke with the first light filtering through the tall windows of his new bedroom, casting a warm glow over the polished wooden floors. He stretched, his muscles protesting slightly from the previous day's activities, along with a slight crick in his neck. The house was quiet, save for the distant ticking of what he assumed was an old clock somewhere – though he hadn't unpacked any clocks yet.

The morning routine felt surreal in the grand old house. His electric toothbrush echoed oddly in the bathroom, making him chuckle. "Good acoustics," he mumbled through toothpaste. "Could start a bathroom choir."

After a quick breakfast, he began his methodical sweep of the house. Box after box awaited his attention, their contents a mystery despite his allegedly organized labeling system. He pulled open one marked "KITCHEN - ESSENTIAL" to find what appeared to be his old college textbooks.

"Right," he sighed, "because nothing says 'essential kitchen items' like Advanced Linguistics." He set the box aside, making a mental note to create a new pile labeled 'Wesley's Organizational Failures.'

Wesley stared at another box, this one marked "Kitchen - FRAGILE" and sighed yet again. "Who packed this?" he muttered, finding his grandmother's porcelain tea set wrapped in what appeared to be his favorite sweaters. "Oh right. I did." He made a mental note to never pack while watching true crime documentaries again.

The fatigue hit him suddenly as he was arranging his grandmother's porcelain in the dining room cabinet. Each piece was still carefully wrapped in bubble wrap, and he found himself having to read the post-it notes he'd stuck on them twice. 'Dessert plates' became 'Desert plates' became 'Plates with the little flowers' as his eyes refused to focus properly.

The grandfather clock in the hallway – which hooked up the weights or pendulum – chimed softly, making him jump. He turned, but there was only empty space where he could have sworn the sound came from. The old house creaked in response, as if sharing a private joke.

"Coffee," he murmured. "I need coffee."

Wesley decided to take a short break, sitting down on one of the dining chairs after starting up the coffee maker. He closed his eyes, taking a few deep breaths as he waited for the pot to finish brewing. The house was silent around him, the only sound the distant ticking of a clock. He rubbed his eyes when the pot finally chimed at him, stepping over to collect his mug and take a few sips.

After a few minutes, he felt a bit better. He stood up, determined to finish at least unpacking the dining room boxes before taking a longer rest. By that point he was due to make a few calls. He reached for another box, his hands steady again.

* * *

Wesley returned from a quick lunch break, his stomach full and his mind clear, ready to tackle the rest of the unpacking. As he stepped into the living room, he paused, his brow furrowing. Something was off. He scanned the room, his gaze landing on the sofa where a familiar sight caught his eye. His parents' favorite art piece, a beautifully framed watercolor of a countryside they had visited on their honeymoon, was leaning against the cushions. He tilted his head, a niggle of unease worming its way into his mind.

"That's odd," he murmured, stepping closer. He was sure he had hung it on the wall opposite the fireplace yesterday, a place of honor where the afternoon light would catch it just right. The picture hooks were still there, which was even weirder. He shook his head, trying to dislodge the creeping discomfort. "Must have forgotten."

Wesley blamed the strange tiredness that had been dogging him since earlier that morning. He had slept a full eight hours last night, yet he felt as if he hadn't rested at all. He chalked it up to the stress of the move and the sheer amount of work still ahead of him - the unpacking, the upcoming visit, and his new job to start in a few weeks after he got settled.

Pushing the thoughts aside, he decided to call the house inspector. He dug out the business card from his wallet and dialed the number, tapping his fingers on the sofa's backrest as he waited for the call to connect.

"Hi, this is Wesley Jameson," he said when the inspector picked up. "I recently purchased the Hawthorne Estate, and you were the one who did the inspection?"

"That's correct," came the reply. "Was there some sort of problem?"

"I was wondering if you could double-check your report for me," Wesley continued. "I've been hearing some strange noises, and I want to make sure every room was thoroughly checked for any potential critters or pests."

There were some scuffling sounds in the background for a few moments before the inspector piped up again.

"Yes, it looks like the house was in really good shape in spite of its age; the electrical wiring and plumbing met regulations, heating and cooling was to standard, and no signs of any nests or burrows on the property."

 "I see." Wesley's gaze drifted back to the art piece. He couldn't shake the feeling that something was amiss.

He thanked them and ended the call, promising to get in touch if he had any more questions, and stood in the silence of the living room, the weight of the house pressing down on him. Could something new have made its way inside? Maybe the doors were left open long enough when the movers were still here; he'd likely have to call animal or pest control, whichever one was good on short notice.

He picked up the art piece, his fingers tracing the familiar frame. The unease grew, gnawing at the edges of his mind. He tried to dismiss it, attributing it to the tiredness and the sheer size of the task ahead. But as he hung the picture back on the wall, the hooks slotting into place with a soft click, he couldn't shake the feeling that he was missing something crucial.

* * *

Wesley glanced out the living room window, his gaze catching the red and blue stripes of the postal service truck as it pulled up to his mailbox. He frowned, setting down the box cutter he'd been using to open another moving box. It seemed a bit early to be receiving mail, considering he'd only just moved in and hadn't yet sorted out things like forwarding his address.

Pushing open the heavy front door, he stepped out onto the porch. The sun was bright, casting sharp shadows across the overgrown lawn. He squinted against the light, making his way down the creaky steps and along the path to the mailbox. The truck was already disappearing down the street by the time he reached it.

Inside the mailbox, he found a small stack of envelopes. Most were addressed to "Current Resident," but one caught his eye. It was a cream-colored envelope, the paper thick and slightly textured, with his full name and new address written in elegant, looping script. He turned it over, finding a wax seal pressed into the back, a stylized "H" imprinted in the red wax. His eyebrows raised, he tucked the envelopes under his arm and headed back towards the house.

As he walked, the crunch of gravel under tires made him look up. A friendly-looking elderly woman was walking towards her own mailbox. She waved at him as she opened the hatch, her gray hair shining silver in the sunlight.

"Afternoon!" she called out, her voice warm and inviting. "You must be the new owner of the Hawthorne Estate. I'm Margaret Wilson, your next-door neighbor."

Wesley offered a smile, adjusting the envelopes under his arm to wave back. "Nice to meet you, Margaret. I'm Wesley Jameson."

Margaret beamed at him, her eyes crinkling at the corners. "A pleasure to meet you, Wesley. I hope you're settling in well?"

He nodded. "Still getting the lay of the land, but it's coming along."

Margaret gestured towards her house. "I was just about to take some fresh-baked cookies out of the oven. Would you like to join me? It'd be a great chance to chat about the neighborhood."

Wesley hesitated for a moment, then nodded. "Sure, that sounds lovely. Thank you."

He followed her into her home, the scent of fresh cookies wafting through the air. Margaret's house was cozy and inviting, filled with the warmth of a well-lived life. Her kitchen was a cozy explosion of floral prints and copper cookware. She bustled around, pulling out what appeared to be her third batch of cookies as Wesley sat at her small kitchen table.

Margaret turned, glancing over at his hands and smiled. "First batch of mail already? That's quick."

Wesley chuckled, setting the stack down on the table as Margaret placed a small plate of cookies in front of him. He gave her a quiet 'thank you' before biting into one, chocolate chip, the warmth comforting. "Most of it isn't for me, just the usual "new or current resident" stuff."

"The neighborhood's quite quiet," she said, sliding another cookie onto his already full plate. "Well, except for the Thompson kids two doors down. Their basketball keeps ending up in my petunias." She paused, studying Wesley's face. "That old house of yours, though... always been a bit of a mystery."

Wesley perked up. "Oh?"

"Mm-hmm," Margaret nodded, already reaching for more cookies. "Been here thirty years, seen people come and go. Never stayed long, mind you. Though that could be because of the property taxes." She winked. "Or the peculiar noises. Old houses, you know how they are."

"Peculiar how?" Wesley asked, accepting another cookie despite himself.

"Oh, just house things. Creaks, groans, the occasional window opening itself..." She waved a hand dismissively. "My Harold – rest his soul – always said old houses were like cats. They do what they want, and you just learn to live with it." She pushed the cookie plate closer. "You look like you could use another one, dear. Moving is such hungry work."

Wesley glanced down at his plate, wondering how he'd accumulated seven cookies without noticing. "Thank you, but I should probably—"

"Nonsense! You're far too skinny. Now, about that garden of yours..."

* * *

Wesley returned from Margaret's house, his mind buzzing with new information and the warmth of fresh cookies. He dove back into unpacking, determined to make a significant dent in the remaining boxes. As he worked, he juggled calls to various pest control services, trying to secure a visit for later in the week. The house creaked and groaned around him, as if echoing his frustration with the endless hold music.

Hours later, Wesley stood in the kitchen, staring at the takeout menus on his phone as he scrolled through his delivery app. "Thai, Chinese, pizza..." he muttered, then glanced guiltily at the full fridge. "Sorry, fresh produce. Tomorrow's your day."

The lights flickered as he reached for his phone. Wesley looked up at the chandelier, raising an eyebrow. "You know, if you're trying to tell me to eat healthier, there are less dramatic ways to do it."

As if in response, the kitchen lights dimmed slightly, then brightened. Wesley chuckled nervously. "Right. Message received. Stir-fry it is."

He pulled out the vegetables he'd bought earlier, the ones that had survived his questionable grocery bag juggling skills. The house's silence felt almost expectant as he chopped and diced, the rhythm of the knife against the cutting board echoing in the large kitchen.

"You know," he said to no one in particular, "I should probably stop talking to the house. People might think I'm..." The lights flickered once, almost playfully. "...exactly as weird as I'm proving to be right now."

Eventually he made his way to the dining room, plate in hand. The grand chandelier overhead cast a warm glow over the polished wooden table. He sat down, the silence of the house pressing in around him. He was about to take his first bite when the lights above flickered briefly again. He paused, fork mid-air, and looked up. The lights steadied, but his brow furrowed.

"Are you trying to tell me something else, now?" He joked. Wesley shrugged when there was no 'response' from the room.

The house seemed to watch him as he ate, its silence almost expectant. He brushed off the feeling, attributing it to the strange tiredness that had been dogging him since the morning. He finished his meal quickly, the sound of his cutlery against the plate echoing in the large room.

As the evening wore on, Wesley wrapped up his unpacking for the day. The boxes were slowly diminishing, but the house still felt vast and empty. He wandered through the rooms, his footsteps echoing on the hardwood floors. He tried to shake off the lingering unease, focusing instead on the promise of a good night's sleep.

He climbed the grand staircase, his hand trailing along the smooth banister. The master bedroom welcomed him, the familiar clutter of his belongings a comfort against the house's grandeur. He changed into his sleep clothes, the routine soothing his frayed nerves.

He took a melatonin tablet, hoping it would guarantee a better night's rest. The house settled around him, its creaks and groans like the sighs of an old friend. He climbed into bed, the cool sheets a stark contrast to the warmth of the day.

His breathing slowed, and the house seemed to breathe with him, its rhythm matching his own. The silence was no longer oppressive but comforting, a lullaby sung by the house itself. And with that thought, Wesley drifted off to sleep.

* * *

Wesley started his day with a quick breakfast and a strong cup of coffee, the rich aroma filling the kitchen. With a newfound energy, he dug through one of the marked boxes in the hallway, fishing out fresh sheets and towels. Today was the day he'd finish setting up the other two bedrooms, a task he'd been putting off. But with Charlie and Teddy's visit looming, he couldn't procrastinate any longer.

The first guest bedroom was bathed in soft morning light, the large windows overlooking the overgrown back garden. Wesley set to work, smoothing out the wrinkles in the linen as he tucked the corners in over the mattress, the rhythmic motion soothing his thoughts. He remembered the countless times he'd done this at his old apartment, the familiarity of the task grounding him in the present.

As he worked, his mind wandered to the upcoming visit. He was looking forward to seeing Charlie and Teddy, their presence a promise of warmth and laughter in the otherwise quiet house. But there was a niggle of worry too. The house was old, and with it came quirks and oddities that he hadn't quite figured out yet. He hoped Charlie and Teddy wouldn't find it too unsettling.

He finished the first bedroom and moved on to the second, his steps echoing in the vast hallway. This room was smaller, cozier, with a view of the wild dandelions and thistle taking over the side yard. He repeated the process, his movements efficient and practiced. As he fluffed the pillows, he heard the crunch of gravel under tires, signaling a car pulling into the driveway.

Wesley glanced out the window, a smile spreading across his face as he recognized Charlie's car. He must have been at this for longer than he thought. He quickly finished up and hurried downstairs. The front door creaked as he pulled it open, revealing Charlie and Teddy, their faces lit up with excitement.

"Uncle Wes!" Teddy exclaimed, bounding up the steps and launching himself at Wesley. Wesley laughed, catching the boy in a hug.

"Hey, buddy! It's great to see you," Wesley said, ruffling Teddy's hair.

Charlie followed, a broad grin on his face. "Wes, good to see you," he said, pulling Wesley into a one-armed hug. "Thanks for having us."

"Thanks for coming," Wesley replied, his voice warm with genuine gratitude. "Let me help you with the bags."

Together, they unloaded the car, the afternoon sun warm on their backs. Teddy chattered excitedly, his eyes wide as he took in the grandeur of the house.

"Uncle Wes," Teddy asked seriously, holding up his stuffed lion, "do your stairs always go creak-creak-meow?"

Wesley blinked. "Meow?"

"Yeah, like a kitty! Listen!" They stood in silence for a moment, but the stairs just creaked normally.

"Must be a special house sound just for you, buddy," Wesley said, exchanging an amused glance with Charlie.

As they began to carry the last of the bags inside, Teddy looked up at one of the windows of the second story and waved. "Hi there!"

Charlie paused a few yards from the front door and glanced at Wesley for a moment before addressing his son. "Teddy, what are you waving at, buddy?"

"Don't you see them, daddy?" Teddy replied, pointing up at the window. "They're saying hi, so we need to say hi back. Grandma says it's polite."

Wesley looked up at where the four year old had indicated and saw nothing there. "Maybe it's his imaginary friend?"

Charlie shook his head. "He has a new one every so often, so it makes sense."

"I want to go say hi, daddy," Teddy told them.

Charlie laughed. "All right, buddy. But we have to finish bringing our stuff in first, okay?"

Teddy beamed up at him. "Okay!"

* * *

"Uncle Wes," Teddy called from the hallway, "your house makes funny noises!"

Wesley looked up from the suitcase he was helping Charlie unpack. "Funny how, buddy?"

"Like..." Teddy scrunched up his face in concentration, "like it's singing! But really quiet. And sometimes it goes tap-tap-tap, like when daddy types really fast on his computer."

Charlie rolled his eyes. "I do not type that loud."

"You do, daddy! Like this!" Teddy demonstrated by dramatically hammering his fingers on an imaginary keyboard, complete with sound effects.

Wesley bit back a laugh. "The house is pretty old, Ted. Old houses make all sorts of sounds."

"I know," Teddy nodded sagely. "She told me."

The temperature in the room seemed to drop a few degrees. Charlie and Wesley exchanged looks.

"Did she... tell you anything else?" Wesley asked carefully.

"She said the house likes to play hide and seek," Teddy replied cheerfully, already distracted by unpacking his toy dinosaurs. "But I told her I'm better at building blocks."

Later that evening, Wesley busied himself in the kitchen, preparing their "guy's night" feast. He popped the pizza rolls and dinosaur nuggets into the toaster oven, the aroma of greasy, delicious junk food filling the air. He hummed to himself as he retrieved the frozen pizzas and curly fries from the freezer.

"Hey, Uncle Wes," Teddy's head popped around the door frame. "Is it done yet?"

Wesley snorted. "Not yet, buddy; I have to cook them in the oven first. Unless you want really cold pizza?"

Teddy made a face at that. "Ew, no! It's supposed to be

melty with the hot cheese on top."

"You're right, Ted," Wesley replied, pouring the fries onto a greased oven tray. "But it's going to be awhile before they're ready. Why don't you go help your dad while I finish everything in here, ok?

"Ok," Teddy chirped, bouncing off towards the living room, Mr. Lion in hand.

Wesley set the table with paper plates and plastic cups around 20 minutes later, a far cry from the elegant dining he'd imagined in this grand room. But tonight, it was perfect. He poured Teddy's juice and grabbed a few cans of soda, the fizzing sound a comforting background noise.

Charlie and Teddy joined him at the table, their faces flushed from their block-building adventures. Wesley served the food, the sizzling pizzas, golden nuggets and fries eliciting delighted squeals from Teddy. They dug in, the clatter of forks and crunch of food punctuating their easy conversation.

Mid-meal, Teddy suddenly paused, his eyes fixed on a point across the room. He waved enthusiastically, a bright smile spreading across his face. "Hi there!" he called out, his voice filled with genuine warmth.

Wesley followed Teddy's gaze, his brow furrowing in confusion. There was nothing there—just an empty wall, the carved details in the wood paneling catching in the dim evening light. He glanced at Charlie, who shrugged, a look of puzzlement mirroring Wesley's own.

"Teddy, who are you waving at, buddy?" Charlie asked, wiping his hands on a napkin.

Teddy looked at them, his eyes wide with innocence.

"The nice people, daddy. They're saying hi too," he explained, as if it were the most natural thing in the world.

"Are they your new friends, Ted?" Wesley asked, glancing between Teddy and the wall again.

"Yes!" He replied. "They waved in the window earlier; can't you see them?"

"Sorry kiddo," Wesley shrugged. "I can't see them either. Are they invisible?"

Teddy laughed, pointing. "No silly! They're right there."

"Okay buddy," Charlie sighed, reaching over to ruffle his son's hair. "If you say so. I guess they're more of your special friends, right?"

"Maybe, they are, daddy."

* * *

Teddy's yawns grew more frequent, his little hands rubbing at his eyes. Charlie pushed his chair back and scooped Teddy up into his arms. "Alright, buddy, let's get you upstairs and into your PJs," he said, planting a kiss on Teddy's forehead. "Uncle Wes and I will be up in a bit to tuck you in, okay?"

"Can Mr. Lion come too?" Teddy mumbled sleepily against his father's shoulder.

"Of course Mr. Lion can come," Charlie smiled, picking up the well-loved stuffed toy. "Say goodnight to Uncle Wes."

"G'night Uncle Wes," Teddy managed through another

yawn. "Don't let the dragons eat all the pizza rolls while I'm sleeping."

Wesley chuckled. "I'll save some just for you, buddy. Sweet dreams."

He smiled, watching as Charlie carried Teddy out of the dining room, the boy's head nestled sleepily on his dad's shoulder. He began clearing the table, the clatter of dishes echoing in the large room. His mind wandered to Teddy's earlier antics, his imaginary friends. It was cute, if a bit peculiar.

He couldn't help but smile at the dinosaur-shaped chicken nugget remains arranged in what Teddy had called a "prehistoric parade" across his plate. The kid's imagination was something else.

Charlie's footsteps on the stairs announced his return. He leaned against the dining room door frame, running a hand through his hair.

"He go down okay?" Wesley asked, gathering empty soda cans.

"Like a light. He always crashes after this much excitement." Charlie moved to help with the cleanup. "Thanks for doing all this, Wes. The guy's night thing... it means a lot to him. To both of us, really."

Wesley waved off the thanks. "Hey, what's the point of having a huge house if you can't share it with your favorite people?" He paused, then added with a grin, "Even if said people eat all my pizza rolls."

"I saw you hoarding that last box," Charlie laughed, then his expression grew more serious. "How are you really doing here, man? And don't give me that 'everything's fine' routine you'd use on your mom."

Wesley stopped, a handful of napkins crumpled in his fist. "Honestly? It's... different. Good different, mostly. But sometimes..." He glanced around the grand dining room, at the shadows playing across the ornate wainscoting. "Sometimes it feels like the house is waiting for something. You know?"

Charlie nodded slowly. "Yeah, old houses can feel like that." He hesitated. "Listen, about what Teddy said earlier, with the waving and everything—"

"Kids have active imaginations," Wesley shrugged, perhaps a bit too quickly. "Remember when you were convinced your aunt's garden gnome was secretly alive?"

"That gnome was definitely evil and no one can convince me otherwise," Charlie deadpanned, then broke into a grin. "But seriously, you'd tell me if anything weird was going on, right?"

"Define weird," Wesley said, trying to keep his tone light. "Because I still can't figure out where half my stuff is, despite my allegedly foolproof labeling system."

"You mean your 'label everything miscellaneous and hope for the best' system?"

"Hey, it worked in college!"

They shared a laugh, the tension easing. Charlie checked his watch. "We should probably head up and check on Ted. He likes one last goodnight before he really falls asleep."

"Lead the way," Wesley said, flicking off the dining room lights. "Though fair warning – if he asks for another bedtime story about the dragon who couldn't sneeze, you're on your own. I used up all my creative juice on that one last time."

* * *

Wesley headed upstairs, Charlie falling into step beside him. The grand staircase creaked under their feet, the house settling around them. They made their way down the hallway, the soft glow of Teddy's nightlight spilling out from the slightly ajar door.

Charlie pushed the door open, revealing Teddy snuggled under the covers, his dark hair a stark contrast against the light pillowcase. His eyes were bright, a wide smile spreading across his face as he looked up at them.

"Hey, buddy," Charlie said, his voice soft. "We're here to tuck you in."

Teddy's smile grew even brighter. "The pretty lady already tucked me in tonight," he declared, his voice filled with childish delight.

Wesley froze, his hand still on the doorknob. He exchanged a glance with Charlie, seeing his own surprise and confusion mirrored in his friend's eyes.

"Pretty lady, Ted?" Charlie asked, his voice careful. "What pretty lady?"

Teddy giggled, pointing towards the far corner of the room. "She was right there. She smiled at me and tucked me in. She's really nice, daddy."

Wesley's gaze followed Teddy's pointing finger as he made his way further into the room, his eyes scanning the empty corner. There was nothing there, just shadows cast by the dim nightlight. He swallowed hard, his mind racing. The house was old, full of creaks and groans, but this... had someone else been up here?

Charlie's hand tightened slightly on the bedspread. "What did the pretty lady look like, Teddy?"

"She has long dark hair," Teddy said through a yawn, snuggling deeper into his pillow. "And a really nice smile. Like in the pictures downstairs."

Wesley felt his stomach drop. He hadn't unpacked any pictures of people yet.

"And she wasn't scared at all when Mr. Lion roared at her," Teddy continued proudly. "She just laughed and said he was very brave to protect me."

Charlie shot Wesley a look that clearly said they'd be discussing this later. "Well, that's... that's good, buddy. But remember what we talked about? About telling Daddy when you meet new people?"

"But she's not new, Daddy," Teddy protested, his eyes already drooping. "She lives here with Uncle Wes. She said so."

The temperature in the room seemed to drop several degrees. Wesley fought the urge to look back over his shoulder at the corner Teddy had pointed to earlier.

"Time for sleep, Ted," Charlie said firmly, tucking the blanket more securely around his son. "Mr. Lion will keep watch, right?"

Teddy nodded, already mostly asleep. "Mm-hmm. G'night Daddy. G'night Uncle Wes." He paused, then mumbled, "G'night pretty lady."

Wesley and Charlie backed out of the room quietly, leaving the door slightly ajar. They stood in the hallway for a moment, the silence heavy between them.

"Wes..." Charlie began.

"Probably just an overactive imagination," Wesley cut in, his voice low. "You know how kids are."

"Yeah," Charlie agreed, but his eyes lingered on Teddy's door. "Yeah, probably."

Neither man mentioned how the hallway lights seemed to dim slightly, as if in response to their conversation.

2

Wesley fumbled with the coffee maker, his exhaustion making the simple task feel like advanced calculus. "I swear this worked yesterday," he muttered, pressing buttons randomly. "The timer was set and everything."

"Maybe it's got a personality like everything else in this house," Charlie said, leaning against the counter. "My microwave at home does this thing where it only works if you shut the door with exactly the right amount of force. Too soft, it pops open. Too hard, it beeps at you judgmentally."

"Judgmentally?" Wesley raised an eyebrow, still fighting with the coffee maker.

"Oh yeah. Three short beeps. Very disapproving." Charlie demonstrated with a surprisingly good impression of microwave beeps. "Like that."

Wesley snorted. "Well, in that case, this coffee maker must be a morning person. Probably judging us for sleeping in." He pressed another button and the machine

28

suddenly sputtered to life, making them both jump. "Ha! See? Just had to sweet talk it a little."

"Great," Charlie yawned. "Now see if you can convince your dishwasher to stop making that weird grinding noise. Kept thinking it was plotting something last night."

"That's just its way of singing along to the radio," Wesley deadpanned. "You should hear it duet with the garbage disposal."

The easy banter helped push back the lingering unease from the previous night, though the lighter mood didn't last as much as either man would have wanted.

"So," Charlie finally began, his voice tentative. He ran a hand through his short-cropped hair, a sign Wesley recognized as his friend's tell for when he was unsettled. "What do you make of Teddy's 'pretty lady'?"

Wesley sighed, wrapping his hands around his mug as if seeking warmth against an unseen chill. "I don't know, Charlie. When we really think about it, it's not like anyone could have gotten in without us noticing. And Teddy's imagination-"

Charlie nodded, taking a sip of his coffee. "Yeah, he's always had a knack for making up friends. But this one... Man, he was so sure, so specific."

Wesley looked out the window, the morning light casting long shadows across the overgrown garden. "Remember when he was convinced that his stuffed bear could talk?"

Charlie chuckled, the tension in his shoulders easing slightly. "Yeah, he was trying to get me into a full-on tea party with it and everything." Charlie shifted his feet. "And it's not like we've seen anything strange ourselves. Maybe it's just the house playing tricks on his mind, old houses and all."

Wesley nodded, though for some reason a niggle of doubt lingered in the back of his mind. He pushed it aside, focusing on the rational explanations. "Let's keep an eye on it, but I don't think we need to worry too much."

Their conversation was interrupted by the sound of small footsteps shuffling down the hallway. Teddy appeared by the door, rubbing his eyes with the back of his hand, his hair tousled from sleep. He looked groggy, his usual bright smile replaced by a grumpy frown.

"Morning, buddy," Charlie said, his voice gentle. "You okay?"

Teddy grumbled something unintelligible and climbed onto Charlie's lap, burying his face in his dad's chest. Charlie looked at Wesley, a concerned furrow in his brow.

"He's not usually like this," Charlie said softly, his hand rubbing circles on Teddy's back. "Maybe he just needs some breakfast."

Wesley got up, grabbing Teddy's favorite cereal from the pantry. He poured a bowl, the colorful loops filling the room with a sugary sweet scent. He placed it in front of Teddy, who looked up with bleary eyes but perked up at the sight of his favorite treat.

"Thanks, Uncle Wes," Teddy mumbled, reaching for the spoon.

As Teddy ate, his grogginess seemed to cling to him like a second skin. His usual chatter was replaced by slow, deliberate chews, his eyes heavy-lidded. Wesley and

Charlie exchanged glances, but neither said a word. They let Teddy eat in silence, the only sound the crunch of cereal and the occasional slurp of milk.

As the morning wore on, Teddy's mood didn't improve. He was cranky, snapping at the smallest things and whining about being tired. Charlie tried to engage him in play, but Teddy just wanted to lie on the couch, his head resting on a pillow.

It wasn't until late afternoon that Teddy finally seemed to shake off his grogginess. He sat up, his eyes clear and bright for the first time that day. He looked around, as if seeing the room for the first time.

"Feeling better, buddy?" Charlie asked, ruffling Teddy's hair.

Teddy nodded, a small smile playing at the corners of his mouth. "Yeah. I had a weird dream, though."

Wesley leaned forward. "What kind of dream, buddy?"

Teddy looked at him, his dark eyes wide. "The pretty lady was in it. She was singing me a song, and it made me sleepy."

Wesley frowned, exchanging a glance with Charlie. He could see his own unease reflected in his friend's eyes. Before either of them could say anything, Teddy hopped off the couch, his energy apparently restored.

"Can we play blocks now, Uncle Wes?" he asked, his voice filled with renewed enthusiasm.

Wesley hesitated for a moment and then nodded, pushing aside his unease. "Sure thing, buddy. Let's go build some towers."

* * *

Wesley sat on the sofa, Teddy nestled between him and Charlie, the glow of the TV casting dancing shadows on their faces. The animated movie played cheerfully, its bright colors a stark contrast to the dimming afternoon light outside. Wesley had suggested the movie hoping it would help them all relax after the strange morning, though he found his attention divided between the screen and Teddy's reactions.

The boy seemed fine now, laughing at all his favorite parts, occasionally reciting lines he'd memorized from previous viewings. Charlie had relaxed too, his earlier tension melting away as he watched his son enjoy the familiar story. The scene felt almost normal; just a family movie afternoon in a slightly too large house.

Then the temperature in the room began to drop.

Wesley noticed it first; a subtle chill that made him pull his sleeves down. He glanced at the others, wondering if they felt it too. Charlie was already reaching for the throw blanket draped over the back of the sofa.

"Getting cold in here," Charlie muttered, spreading the blanket over Teddy's lap. "Must be the old heating system acting up again."

"The house came with those upgraded." Wesley replied, glancing down at his phone. "I'll check the thermostat a bit later; my app's telling me it's still set at 75."

"Is this set up with smart home stuff?"

"No. I've thought about it, though."

It wasn't just that the room was cold. There was something else, something Wesley couldn't quite put his finger on. It had grown quieter, though the TV still played at the same volume. It was the kind of stillness that made the hair on the back of your neck stand up, the kind that made you want to look over your shoulder even though you knew no one was there.

The animated characters on screen were in the middle of their usual end-of-episode song when Teddy went rigid beside him. The boy's small body tensed, his hands gripping the edge of the blanket so tightly his knuckles turned white. His eyes, wide and unblinking, fixed on a point somewhere in the empty space before them.

Wesley felt the abrupt change in Teddy's demeanor like an electric shock. He exchanged a worried glance with Charlie, who had also noticed the sudden shift. The cheerful song continued to play, its upbeat melody now feeling jarringly out of place in the heavy silence that had fallen over them.

The shadows in the corners of the room seemed to deepen, though Wesley told himself it was just the natural progression of the afternoon sun. The house creaked, an ordinary sound he'd heard a hundred times before, but now it felt different – more deliberate somehow.

"Teddy?" Charlie's voice was gentle yet laced with worry, breaking through the strange stillness. "What's wrong, buddy?"

Teddy didn't respond. His eyes remained fixed, unblinking, on that empty space. A shiver ran through his small frame, visible even under the blanket. Wesley could feel the tension radiating off him, could see the fear that seemed to grip him. It was unlike anything he had seen from the usually cheerful four-year-old.

The credits began to roll on screen, the bright animation creating strange, shifting patterns of light and shadow in the room. Wesley leaned in closer, a bit shaky himself. He could feel the cold more intensely now, as if it was seeping into his bones.

"Teddy, talk to us," Wesley urged, his voice soft but firm. He placed a comforting hand on Teddy's shoulder, feeling the tremble beneath his touch. "What do you see, buddy?"

Teddy's lips parted slightly, as if he were about to speak, but no sound came out. His eyes remained locked on that same spot, his breath coming in shallow gasps. Wesley and Charlie exchanged another glance, the worry in their eyes deepening. The silence stretched between them, broken only by the cheerful tune of the movie's end credits, now seeming almost mocking in its brightness.

The room grew colder still.

Then, Teddy's eyes finally flickered, breaking away from the empty space to look up at his father. His lips trembled.

"I can't breathe."

* * *

Wesley's heart pounded as he and Charlie swiftly checked Teddy over, their hands gentle yet hurried as they felt for any obstruction, any sign that something was physically wrong. Teddy's breathing eventually seemed to ease, his small chest rising and falling steadily, but the fear in his eyes remained.

"I think he's okay," Wesley murmured, his voice barely above a whisper, as if speaking too loudly might shatter the fragile calm that had settled over Teddy.

Charlie nodded; his brow furrowed in concern as he pulled out his phone. "I'm taking him to the pediatrician. It looks like there's one not too far from here. I want to make sure he's really alright."

Wesley nodded in agreement, understanding the urgency in Charlie's voice. "I'll stay here, just in case... just in case there's something else going on."

Charlie scooped Teddy up into his arms, the boy's head resting on his shoulder. Wesley could see the fear lingering in Teddy's eyes, but there was also trust; knowledge that his dad would make things right. It made Wesley's heart ache.

He walked them to the door, the cool evening air a stark contrast to the warmth of the front hallway. He stood by the front door and watched as Charlie buckled Teddy into his car seat, the boy's eyes never leaving Wesley until the car pulled out of the driveway and disappeared down the road.

Wesley remained there for a moment, the quiet of the night settling around him before finally heading back to the kitchen, footsteps echoing slightly on the hardwood floor. He began to tidy up, needing something to keep his hands busy. He opened the cupboard to put away the box of cereal they'd left out, and that's when he saw it.

Scrawled in dark, stark letters across the inside of the cupboard door was a message: "Where is Larry?"

Wesley froze, his heart pounding in his chest. He blinked, hoping it was just a trick of the light, a figment of his imagination. But the words remained, etched into the wood as if burned there.

He reached out a tentative hand, his fingers tracing the letters. The ink felt cold, sending a shiver down his spine. He quickly pulled his hand away, a sense of unease washing over him.

He opened another cupboard, then another, finding the same message scrawled in each one. "Where is Larry?" It was like a macabre game of hide and seek, the house taunting him with its cryptic question.

Wesley's mind raced as he stood there, staring at the message. His mind immediately started cataloging possibilities: Vandalism? No signs of forced entry. Previous owners? The inspection hadn't mentioned any graffiti, and he'd opened these same cupboards earlier that day. A prank? But who would have access to every cabinet without alerting either of them if they were there?

He reached for his phone to Google "Larry Hawthorne" before stopping himself. "Great," he muttered. "Now I'm turning into one of those ghost hunting streamers."

As Wesley stood there in the empty kitchen, the silence pressing in around him, he had one major question:

"Who's Larry?"

* * *

Wesley checked everywhere he could think of: the locks on the doors, the latches on the windows, for any sign, just to be completely sure. There were no signs of forced entry, no evidence of anyone else in the house except himself - just as he'd initially thought. The Hawthorne Estate was as silent and undisturbed as it had been when he first set foot inside.

The sound of a car pulling into the driveway made him jump. Through the window, he saw Charlie's car, the headlights casting long shadows across the lawn. He stepped outside, the cool evening air a stark contrast to the tension inside the house.

Charlie got out of the car, Teddy cradled in his arms. The boy looked sleepy but calm, his head resting on his father's shoulder. Wesley felt a wave of relief wash over him at the sight of them, safe and unharmed.

"How was the pediatrician?" Wesley asked, his voice steady despite the turmoil inside him.

"Clean bill of health," Charlie replied, adjusting Teddy in his arms. "Though I may have slightly panicked at the pharmacy afterward."

Wesley raised an eyebrow as Charlie shifted Teddy to one arm and held up not one but three bulging shopping bags. "Slightly panicked?"

"I bought tea," Charlie said defensively.

"You bought... tea."

"Herbal tea. For calming." Charlie followed Wesley into the house. "And sleeping. And relaxing. And whatever else they had labels for."

Wesley peered into one of the bags. "Charlie, did you buy the entire tea aisle?"

"The cashier was very helpful," Charlie muttered. "She kept suggesting different blends. Did you know they make tea specifically for midnight anxiety? And one for 'spiritual cleansing'? I drew the line at the one that promised to align your chakras."

Wesley bit back a laugh. "So, what you're telling me is that somewhere in these bags is the solution to all our problems, provided our problems can be solved by aggressive hydration?"

"Hey man, my mother swears by this stuff," Charlie protested, but a smile was tugging at the corners of his mouth. "Though she might have forgotten to mention how many cups you need to drink before you start seeing results. Or stop seeing things, in our case."

Teddy stirred in Charlie's arms, blinking sleepily. "Can I have the strawberry one?"

"Sure, buddy," Charlie said, then added in a stage whisper to Wesley: "At least someone appreciates my panic shopping."

Wesley helped Charlie settle Teddy on the couch, tucking a blanket around him. As he watched the boy curl up with his stuffed lion, looking perfectly normal and peaceful, the weight of what he'd discovered in the kitchen pressed heavily on his mind.

"Charlie," he said quietly, "there's something you need to see. In the kitchen."

Charlie looked up from where he was arranging his tea collection on the coffee table, his expression growing serious at Wesley's tone. "What is it?"

"It's... well, it's easier if I show you." Wesley glanced at Teddy, who was already dozing off. "You might want to leave the calming tea out. We're probably going to need it."

They made their way to the kitchen, leaving Teddy sleeping soundly on the couch. The house seemed to hold its breath as Wesley reached for the cabinet door, the creak of its hinges unnaturally loud in the quiet room.

Charlie stared at the dark message scrawled inside, his eyes widening. "Where is Larry?" he read aloud, his voice barely above a whisper.

"It's in all of them," Wesley said, opening another cabinet, then another. "Every single one."

Charlie ran a hand through his hair, his earlier humor forgotten. "Well," he said finally, "I guess we know why the spiritual cleansing tea was on sale."

"Maybe we need stronger tea to deal with this," Wesley joked weakly, trying to break the tension.

Charlie chuckled, but the sound was hollow, lacking any real humor. "Yeah, maybe. Or something stronger in the tea."

They both stared at the messages, the same three words repeated over and over, like a question that demanded to be answered. The house creaked around them, its usual settling sounds now carrying a weight of expectation.

"Should I grab a bottle?" Wesley asked.

"Please."

* * *

Wesley watched Charlie pull out his phone, his fingers

dancing across the screen as he typed in a search query. A half empty bottle of scotch and two tumblers rested on the counter next to them.

"Okay, let's see how to get rid of this ink," Charlie muttered, his eyes scanning the search results. Wesley leaned against the counter, his arms crossed over his chest, a sense of unease still gnawing at him. He reached for one of the tumblers and took a swig out of it to take the edge off.

Charlie's brow furrowed as he scrolled through the results. "Huh, that's weird," he said, his voice laced with confusion. "I'm getting some strange suggestions here."

Wesley raised an eyebrow, putting his glass down. "Strange how?"

Charlie looked up from his phone, a smirk playing at the corners of his mouth. "Well, according to these forums, we're not the only ones dealing with 'unfamiliar writing' and..." he paused, his smirk growing into a full-blown grin, "hauntings."

Wesley scoffed, rolling his eyes. "Hauntings? Really, Charlie?"

Charlie chuckled, turning his phone towards Wesley. "See for yourself, man. There are whole threads dedicated to this stuff. People sharing their experiences, offering advice."

Wesley took the phone as Charlie reached for the other glass and took a sip, his eyes scanning the forum posts. He couldn't help but chuckle at some of the more outlandish suggestions. "Sprinkle salt around the house? Sage? Really?"

Charlie laughed, taking his phone back. "Yeah, and listen to this one," he said, his voice taking on a dramatic flair. "'Communicate with the spirit. Ask it what it wants. Maybe it just wants to be heard.'"

Wesley burst out laughing, the tension in his chest easing slightly. "Oh, that's brilliant. Maybe we should set up a Ouija board, have a little chat with our ink-loving friend."

Charlie joined in the laughter, the sound filling the kitchen, pushing back the unease that had settled over them. "Or how about this one," Charlie continued, his voice growing bolder with each suggestion. "'Play music that was popular when the spirit was alive. Maybe it'll trigger a memory and make it move on.'"

Wesley leaned back against the counter, a smile still on his face. "Well, that's a new one. I've heard of using music to soothe the savage beast, but the savage ghost?"

Charlie chuckled, scrolling through more of the forum posts. "Oh, here's a good one. 'Leave out an offering. Food, drink, something the spirit might have liked in life.'"

Wesley raised an eyebrow, his smile fading slightly. "An offering, huh? You think our ghost has a sweet tooth?"

Charlie looked up from his phone, a thoughtful expression on his face. "Well, it couldn't hurt, right? And who knows, maybe it'll like Teddy's favorite cereal."

Wesley shook his head, a wry smile playing at the corners of his mouth. "I can't believe we're even considering this, Charlie. We're grown men, talking about leaving out offerings for ghosts."

Charlie shrugged, a mischievous glint in his eye as he held his tumbler up. "Hey man, when in Rome, right? Or in this case, when in the Hawthorne Estate."

Wesley chuckled, pushing off from the counter to clink his glass against Charlie's. The laughter and booze had helped, the tension in his chest easing, the unease in his gut lessening. But the questions still lingered, the mystery of the messages, the strange occurrences, the unknown.

"Alright, Charlie," Wesley said, a determined look in his eye. "Let's see if our ghost has a taste for sugary cereal."

* * *

Things got a bit sidetracked as the pair consumed the rest of the scotch and replaced it with another; the tension from earlier had completely melted away. In the meantime, Wesley had found an old Ouija board tucked away in one of his boxes and the two became quickly occupied with it.

After about an hour of asking a mixture strange and ridiculous questions with it while messing around with the little view-glass, Charlie held up the Ouija board, squinting at it through his third glass of scotch. "You think we should ask about Larry?"

"Nah," Wesley waved his hand dismissively. "Let's ask something important, like... does the ghost know where I packed my phone charger?"

They both laughed, but the sound died quickly as the lights flickered overhead.

"Maybe we should stick to cereal offerings," Charlie suggested, setting the board aside.

"Good idea," Wesley replied, turning to pull out one of

the colorful boxes from the pantry behind him.

It wasn't long before the two of them were standing in the dimly lit kitchen, the only sound the soft ticking of the vintage clock on the wall. They looked down at the circle of cereal they had laid out on the counter, a smirk playing on both their faces.

"You think we should say some magic words or something?" Charlie asked, his voice laced with sarcasm. He waved his hands over the cereal like a mock magician. "Abracadabra, alakazam?"

Wesley chuckled, shaking his head. "I think if our ghost has a sense of humor, it's probably rolling its eyes at us right about now." He picked up a piece of cereal and popped it into his mouth, crunching loudly. "Maybe it just needs to see that we're enjoying the offering first."

Charlie laughed, grabbing a handful of cereal for himself. "To the ghost with good taste," he said, raising the cereal like a toast before tossing it into his mouth.

They stood there for a moment, chewing and laughing, the tension from earlier dissipating into the night.

Once the laughter subsided, Wesley looked back down at the cereal. His smile faded, replaced by a thoughtful frown. "You know, part of me actually wishes something would happen," he confessed, his voice barely above a whisper.

Charlie snorted. "It'd certainly be something different."

Wesley nodded and glanced at the clock, noting the late hour. "We should get some sleep. Maybe things will be different in the morning."

Charlie agreed. With a brief stop at the living room couch to collect Teddy, they both headed upstairs, leaving the circle of cereal untouched on the counter.

Hours later, Wesley found himself wide awake, staring at the ceiling. The house was quiet, too quiet. He sighed, kicking off the covers and swinging his legs out of bed. Sleep was clearly not on his side tonight.

He found himself creeping downstairs, trying to prevent the floorboards from creaking under his feet. The last thing he needed was to rouse Teddy from his bed; the kid needed all the sleep he could get. The kitchen was bathed in the silver glow of moonlight, casting long, dancing shadows across the room.

The cereal was exactly as they'd left it on the counter, a near perfect circle in the moonlight. Wesley let out a breath, a mixture of relief and disappointment washing over him. He wasn't sure what he had expected, but this was somehow anticlimactic.

A soft creak behind him made him jump. He spun around, his heart leaping into his throat. Charlie stood in the doorway, rubbing his eyes sleepily.

"Couldn't sleep either, huh?" Charlie asked, his voice groggy.

Wesley shook his head, a wry smile playing on his lips. "Guess not."

Charlie walked over to the counter, his eyes landing on the cereal. He let out a soft chuckle, looking up at Wesley with a knowing glance. "Well, at least we know our ghost isn't a cereal fan."

Wesley laughed.

* * *

Wesley stood by the counter, coffee in hand, watching as Charlie picked up the remnants of their late-night cereal circle. The morning light streaming through the window gave the kitchen a warm, comforting glow, a stark contrast to the eerie atmosphere of the night before. He took a sip of his coffee, the rich aroma grounding him in the present, pushing away the lingering unease.

Charlie looked up from his task, a smirk playing at the corners of his mouth. "You know, Wes, if anyone had told me I'd be cleaning up cereal offerings for a ghost, I'd have laughed in their face."

Wesley chuckled, setting his coffee down on the counter. "Well, it's not exactly how I imagined starting my day either."

The sound of small footsteps echoed down the hall, and Teddy entered the kitchen, rubbing his eyes sleepily. "Morning," he mumbled, his voice still heavy with sleep.

Charlie turned, a wide smile spreading across his face. "Morning, buddy!" He scooped Teddy up into his arms, the boy giggling as Charlie spun him around in a full good-morning hug.

Teddy's eyes landed on the cereal scattered across the counter, his brow furrowing in confusion. "Why's there cereal on the table?" he asked, pointing at the mess.

Charlie laughed, turning to face the cereal. "Well, buddy, we were just—" He stopped mid-sentence, his eyes widening in disbelief.

Wesley followed Charlie's gaze and couldn't help but gasp. One of the pieces of cereal had vanished, leaving a small gap in the circle. He blinked, rubbing his eyes, sure that he was seeing things. But the cereal was definitely gone.

Teddy laughed, a sound of pure delight filling the kitchen. "She's eating the cereal!" he exclaimed, clapping his hands together.

Wesley and Charlie exchanged a look, a mix of shock and confusion passing between them. Wesley stepped forward, his eyes scanning around the counter and on the floor, searching for any sign of the missing cereal. But it was gone, vanished into thin air.

Teddy wiggled in Charlie's arms, eager to be put down. Charlie complied, setting the boy down gently on one of the kitchen chairs. Teddy immediately leaned over the counter to see the cereal, his eyes wide with wonder as he pointed at the gap.

"She likes it!" Teddy declared, looking up at Wesley and Charlie with an enthusiastic bounce on the seat.

Charlie's stern 'Don't jump on the furniture' was ignored by the four year old.

Wesley forced a smile, the sight of Teddy's joy pushing back the unease. He ruffled the boy's hair, a gentle, affectionate gesture. "I guess she does, buddy. And your dad's right; if you bounce on my chairs they might break. "

"You might hurt yourself, too, Ted," Charlie added. "This is Wesley's house; you need to be nice to his stuff, okay?"

"Oh," Teddy blinked, pausing mid-bounce. "Sorry, Uncle Wes. I won't jump on them anymore."

"Thanks, buddy." Wesley replied. "My chairs thank you, too."

As Wesley looked back at the cereal, the gap where one piece had vanished, he couldn't shake the feeling of unease. Something was happening and they were right in the middle of it.

* * *

Wesley sat on the living room floor, a half-eaten sandwich forgotten on the plate beside him. His attention was fixed on Teddy, who sat cross-legged by the fireplace, chattering away to what appeared to be empty air. But there was something different about this compared to the boy's usual imaginary conversations, something that made the hair on Wesley's neck stand up.

"But why can't Uncle Wes see you?" Teddy asked, his head tilted in that peculiar way children do when they're processing new information. He nodded seriously, as if receiving a particularly important answer. "Oh. Is that why you're sad sometimes?"

Wesley exchanged a look with Charlie, who had abandoned any pretense of reading his book on the couch. These weren't the usual imaginative ramblings of a four-year-old. Teddy's typical make-believe friends were dinosaurs or superheroes, not... whatever this was.

"The pretty lady says she likes your house, Uncle Wes," Teddy announced suddenly, making both men jump. "But she thinks you should fix the music room."

Wesley frowned. "Music room?"

"The one upstairs with the piano," Teddy said matter-of-factly. "Behind the door that's stuck."

Charlie sat up straighter. "Teddy, how do you know about a piano?"

"She showed me." Teddy shrugged, as if this was the most natural thing in the world. "In my dream last night. She was playing it, but the notes were all wrong because it's been sleeping too long."

Wesley felt a chill run down his spine. There had been a space in the wall that looked like it would fit a door there during his tour with the realtor, and she hadn't mentioned anything about it, so he'd chalked it up to being some sort of weird design thing for older houses. Those don't always have uniform measurements for everything.

But what if there used to be a door? Outside of the official tour he hadn't even fully explored the upper floor yet, still focused on unpacking the essential rooms. How would he know that, though, when Wesley had no clue himself? Teddy's attention shifted back to his unseen companion, his small face scrunching in concentration.

"Uncle Wes," Teddy said suddenly, his voice taking on that serious tone children use when delivering what they consider vital information. "She says the house misses music. Like she does." He paused, as if listening. "And she says you should check the attic. There's something important up there."

Important? Wesley opened his mouth to ask, but the boy returned to his blocks as if he hadn't said anything unusual, humming a tune neither man recognized. Wesley and Charlie exchanged looks, the same questions reflecting in their eyes. What else did this "pretty lady" tell him about the house?

The afternoon light seemed to dim slightly, though no clouds crossed the sun outside. Wesley shivered, suddenly aware of how quiet the house had become, as if it too was listening to Teddy's strange conversation.

Teddy continued his conversation, apparently oblivious to the adults' discomfort. "No, I won't tell them that part," he giggled.

The temperature in the room seemed to drop several degrees.

* * *

The pest control representative's footsteps echoed through the hallway, each sound seeming to highlight the vastness of the house. Wesley followed behind as he asked questions, watching as the flashlight beam cut through shadows in those tight crawl spaces that seemed to grow darker the moment the light moved on.

"Well, Mr. Jameson," the rep said, clicking off his flashlight, "I've checked every possible entry point. No signs of rodents, no evidence of nests, not even a spider web. Which, I've got to say, is pretty unusual for a house this old."

Wesley nodded, trying to ignore the way the shadows seemed to shift in his peripheral vision. "So, nothing could have gotten in? No animals at all?"

"Not unless they've learned to pick locks," the rep chuckled. "You've got some solid construction here. Even the original windowsills are intact, no gaps or..."

His voice trailed off as Charlie's shout echoed from the

living room. "Wes! You need to see this!"

Wesley rushed toward the sound, his heart pounding. He rounded the corner to find Teddy standing in the middle of the room, soaking wet, his clothes dripping onto the hardwood floor. The boy swayed slightly, his eyes unfocused, as if he'd just woken from a deep sleep.

"I was only gone for a minute," Charlie said, his voice tight with worry. "He was playing with his blocks, I went to get his juice, and when I came back..."

Wesley knelt beside Teddy as Charlie ran off to grab a towel and dry clothes, gently touching the boy's arm. His skin was cold; pajamas completely drenched. Behind him, he heard the pest control rep let out a low whistle.

As they helped Teddy out of his wet clothes, Wesley's mind raced. The bathroom sink was found to be dry, untouched. No running taps, no splashed water on the floor. It was as if Teddy had been dunked in water that didn't exist.

"The lady wanted to show me the fish," Teddy mumbled sleepily as Charlie wrapped him in a towel.

"What fish, buddy?" Charlie asked, his voice carefully controlled.

"The ones in the lake," Teddy yawned. "She says they used to swim here, before the ground got hungry and ate all the water."

Wesley felt his stomach drop. "Lake? What lake, Teddy?"

But the boy was already drifting off, his head drooping against Charlie's shoulder. Charlie gathered him closer, looking at Wesley with concern. "There's no lake on your property, right?"

"No," Wesley said slowly, thinking back to his property tour. "The real estate agent walked me through everything. There's the garden in the back, the old greenhouse shed, that overgrown tennis court... but no lake." He ran a hand through his hair, frustrated. "I would have remembered a lake."

The pest control rep cleared his throat, reminding them of his presence. "Actually," he said, shifting uncomfortably, "lot of these old estates used to have water features. Lakes, ponds... my grandfather used to talk about them. Most got filled in during development booms, turned into extra land for housing and such."

Wesley turned to stare at him. "You think there used to be a lake here?"

The man shrugged. "Could be. Records office might know. They keep maps going way back." He glanced at Teddy, then at the wet floor, and took a step toward the door. "I'll just... finish up my report in the truck."

After the rep left, Charlie settled Teddy on the couch in his fresh clothes and a blanket. The boy curled up immediately, clutching his stuffed lion close. Wesley couldn't stop staring at the water marks on the floor, perfectly round drops that seemed to lead nowhere.

"I should check the property records," Wesley said quietly. "Find out if there really was a lake here."

Charlie nodded, his hand resting protectively on Teddy's head. "Yeah. Yeah, that might be good." He paused, then added, "But Wes? Maybe don't mention the whole 'ground got hungry' thing when you ask."

* * *

The TV droned on quietly in the background, but neither Wesley nor Charlie was paying attention to it. They sat in the kitchen, surrounded by Charlie's collection of herbal teas, each lost in their own thoughts.

"We need to talk about what's happening," Wesley finally said, breaking the silence. "Really talk about it."

Charlie nodded, wrapping his hands around his mug of "Extra Calming Chamomile" as if seeking warmth. "Yeah. Yeah, we do."

"The messages in the cabinets, Teddy's mysterious friend, the water incident..." Wesley ticked off each event on his fingers. "Charlie, I'm starting to think..."

"That we're dealing with something we can't explain?" Charlie finished. "Yeah, I got there right around the time my son started having conversations with someone only he can see about rooms we didn't know existed."

They sat in silence for a moment, letting the weight of their words settle around them. The house creaked, a sound that seemed more meaningful now than ever.

"You know what's weird?" Wesley said, staring into his own cup of tea. "I keep thinking about that letter I got. The one with the fancy seal."

"The weird letter? What about it?"

"I never opened it." Wesley ran a hand through his hair. "It's still sitting on my dresser upstairs. I meant to, but then everything started happening, and..."

A soft thud from upstairs interrupted him. They both froze, listening. The sound came again, followed by the unmistakable sound of Teddy's voice.

They found him in his room, sitting up in bed, his eyes closed but his mouth moving in conversation. The voice that came out wasn't Teddy's - it was higher, softer, with an accent that belonged to another time.

"The music needs to come back," said the strange voice through Teddy's mouth. "The house has been quiet for too long."

Wesley and Charlie stood frozen in the doorway, their breath visible in the suddenly cold air. Teddy's night light flickered, casting strange shadows on the walls.

"The music?" Wesley managed to ask, his voice barely a whisper.

Teddy's head turned toward them, his eyes still closed. When he spoke again, it was still in that unfamiliar voice: "In the attic. I left it in the attic, waiting. Like everything else."

The night light went out, plunging the room into darkness. When it flickered back on seconds later, Teddy was lying down, sleeping peacefully as if nothing had happened. But on the wall above his bed, written in what looked like water stains, was a single word:

"Remember."

3

Wesley sat on the edge of his bed, the events of the night replaying in his mind like a fever dream. The word "Remember" had faded from Teddy's wall, leaving no trace it had ever been there, which somehow made everything worse. He looked at Charlie, who was wearing a path into the carpet with his pacing.

"You know," Wesley said, attempting to inject some normalcy into the surreal situation, "if you keep that up, I'm going to have to replace the carpet before I even finish unpacking."

Charlie paused mid-stride, a ghost of a smile crossing his face before fading. "Sorry. It's just... what do you do when your parenting books don't cover 'my son might be channeling spirits'?"

"Check the supernatural parenting section online?" Wesley suggested, earning a weak chuckle from his friend.

Charlie finally stopped pacing and turned to face Wesley,

his expression serious. "I don't know, Wes. I think it's time we stop pretending this is just old house quirks or an overactive imagination. This is something..." he gestured vaguely, "beyond our understanding."

Wesley nodded slowly. "You mean something actually supernatural?" The seriousness of the words felt strange on his tongue, like speaking a foreign language.

"I don't know what to call it," Charlie sighed, running a hand through his short-cropped hair. "But I know that what's happening to Teddy isn't normal. And it seems to be centered on him."

Wesley thought back to the past few days: Teddy's conversations with his invisible friend, the disappearing cereal, the strange voice that wasn't his. Each incident on its own could be explained away, but together they formed a pattern that was impossible to ignore.

"But where do we start?" Charlie continued, his voice tight with worry. "We don't know anything about this stuff, Wes. The closest either of us has come to paranormal research is binge-watching those ghost hunting shows in college."

"Hey, I'll have you know I learned a lot from those shows," Wesley protested, then grew serious. "We start with the house. We need to find out about the previous inhabitants, about the history of this place."

Charlie's face brightened slightly. "Right. If something happened here in the past, maybe it's affecting what's happening now. It's a start, at least."

"We'll start first thing in the morning," Wesley said, then added with forced lightness, "After coffee. Lots of coffee."

"Agreed." Charlie smiled, but it didn't reach his eyes. "Think your ghost takes requests? Could really use an ethereal barista right about now."

Wesley snorted. "With our luck, we'd end up with some Victorian-era tea snob judging our coffee preferences."

* * *

Wesley sat at the kitchen table, his laptop open in front of him, the scent of freshly brewed coffee filling the air. He took a sip from his mug, the hot liquid grounding him as he navigated through various online databases, searching for any information related to the house. Teddy's imaginary friend wouldn't leave his mind; it was a puzzle piece that didn't quite fit anywhere yet.

The sound of footsteps pulled him from his thoughts, and he looked up to see Charlie entering the room. His friend headed straight for the coffee maker, pouring himself a cup before turning to face Wesley.

"Any luck with the search?" Charlie asked, taking a sip of his coffee.

Wesley sighed, leaning back in his chair. "I've put in a query for census information, but it's going to take a while to get a response. It's the weekend, so the census department isn't exactly rushing to answer."

Charlie nodded, pulling out a chair to sit beside Wesley. "Makes sense. Guess we'll just have to be patient."

Wesley's fingers hovered over the keyboard as he tried different search combinations: "Hawthorne Estate history," "Hawthorne house deaths," "Hawthorne property records." Each search brought up fragments of information, but nothing substantial enough to explain what was happening.

"Listen to this," he said, turning the laptop slightly. "Apparently the house was built in 1856 by Alexander Hawthorne for his wife Eleanor. They had three children and... that's it. The rest is just property tax records and renovation permits."

"Riveting," Charlie mumbled into his coffee cup. "Think Eleanor's ghost has strong opinions about your kitchen cabinets?"

Wesley was about to reply when Teddy shuffled in, looking even more exhausted than the previous day. The boy's usual morning chatter was replaced with a quiet that felt wrong, like a song playing off-key.

"Hey, sunshine," Charlie said softly, pulling Teddy into his lap. "Not feeling great?"

Teddy just shook his head, burrowing into his father's chest. Charlie met Wesley's eyes over his son's head, worry clear in his expression.

"Have you found anything about kids getting sick in the house?" Charlie asked quietly as he stroked Teddy's hair.

Wesley shook his head, frustration evident in his voice. "Nothing specific. Though it's not like 'house makes child mysteriously tired' would make it into the official records."

Teddy stirred slightly. "She says the house isn't making me sick," he mumbled against Charlie's shirt.

Both men froze. Wesley leaned forward carefully. "Who says that, Teddy?"

But Teddy had already drifted off again, his breathing even and deep. Charlie tightened his hold on his son, his jaw clenched with worry.

"I'm calling his pediatrician again," Charlie said, though they both knew what the doctor would say; nothing was physically wrong with Teddy.

Wesley watched as Charlie shifted Teddy to a more comfortable position, noting how the morning light seemed to pass straight through the boy's skin, making him look almost transparent. He quickly blinked and looked again; Teddy was solid as ever. Just tired. Very tired.

He turned back to his laptop, adding "Hawthorne Estate disappearances" to his growing list of searches, trying not to think about why that particular phrase had come to mind.

* * *

Wesley's eyes burned from staring at his laptop screen, but he couldn't stop scrolling. The local history groups had accepted his join requests with surprising speed; apparently, having the Hawthorne Estate as his listed address opened digital doors.

"You know what's weird?" he said, breaking the concentrated silence. "I can find plenty about the house being built, about renovations, about property values... but almost nothing about the families who lived here."

Charlie looked up from his phone, where he'd been deep in another parenting forum. "Maybe they were just private people?"

"For over a hundred and fifty years?" Wesley shook his head. "It's strange. There are plenty of property records, but when it comes to actual residents, it's like looking at a half-finished puzzle. The Hawthornes haven't lived here since the 1890s, but various relatives have tried to move in over the years."

"Tried to?" Charlie asked, his attention caught.

"Yeah. According to these forums, none of them stayed longer than a few months. No explanation why, they just... left." Wesley ran a hand through his hair. "The posts are full of speculation but nothing concrete. Just vague rumors about the house being 'unwelcoming' to new residents."

Charlie leaned forward to look at the screen. "But someone must know something. Houses this old usually have tons of history."

"That's just it," Wesley said, scrolling through another forum thread. "Outside of basic census records, which we're still waiting on, there's barely anything about the families who tried to live here. It's like..." he paused, searching for the right words, "like the house didn't want them remembered."

They both glanced around the kitchen, the morning light suddenly seeming a little dimmer. The house creaked, its usual settling sounds taking on a different meaning in the wake of their conversation.

"Well, that's not ominous at all," Charlie muttered, reaching for his coffee cup.

"What about the mom groups?" Wesley asked, trying to shift focus.

Charlie snorted, though it sounded forced. "Oh, I've found plenty. Did you know that sudden fatigue in children could be caused by everything from gluten to solar flares to negative energy from old furniture?"

"Seriously?"

"MommaBear78 is very convinced about the furniture thing. She recommended something called 'energetic cleansing' using..." Charlie squinted at his phone, "crystal-infused moon-water."

Despite the situation, Wesley couldn't help but laugh. "Please tell me you're not considering that."

"Hey, at this point?" Charlie gestured around the house. "Crystal moon-water isn't even in the top ten weirdest things happening here."

* * *

Wesley watched as Teddy curled up in his usual spot by the fireplace, talking animatedly to thin air despite his obvious exhaustion. The boy's energy seemed to come in waves now - moments of almost manic alertness followed by periods of bone-deep fatigue.

"Evelyn knows lots of stories," Teddy said, his eyes bright with an unnatural fever-like gleam. "She says this house is full of them."

Charlie, who had been pretending to read a book while actually watching his son like a hawk, lowered it slowly. "What kind of stories, buddy?"

"About the music," Teddy said, his voice taking on an odd, distant quality. "About the piano that used to sing every evening. About the little boy who loved to dance to it." He paused, head tilted as if listening. "She says the house misses the music."

Wesley felt goosebumps rise on his arms. The house had been silent since they arrived, except for their own noise and its natural creaks and groans. But now, listening to Teddy, he could almost imagine the ghostly echo of piano keys.

"The house was so happy then," Teddy continued, his eyes growing heavy. "Before the water came. Before the ground got hungry."

Charlie moved to the fireplace, kneeling beside his son. "Teddy, how do you know about a piano? About the music?"

"Evelyn shows me," Teddy mumbled, fighting to keep his eyes open. "In my dreams. She says... she says the house remembers everything."

Teddy nodded as if this made perfect sense. "Evelyn says she'll tell me a story now. About this house, and about a secret." His voice took on an odd, sing-song quality. "About the music room and the lake and why the ground got hungry."

Wesley and Charlie exchanged alarmed looks. Before either could respond, Teddy's eyes fluttered closed, his small body slumping sideways.

Charlie was there in an instant, gathering his son into his arms. "Teddy? Buddy?"

"'m just tired," Teddy mumbled. "Evelyn's stories make me sleepy sometimes."

As Charlie carried Teddy to the couch, Wesley couldn't shake the feeling that they were missing something obvious. The house, the secret, the lake; it was all connected somehow, but the pattern kept slipping away like water through his fingers.

"I don't like this, Wes," Charlie said softly, brushing Teddy's hair back from his forehead. "He's getting worse."

"I don't either," Wesley agreed. Whatever was happening to Teddy was accelerating, drawing him deeper into whatever mystery the Estate was hiding.

The house creaked around them, its familiar settling sounds somehow more purposeful than before. Wesley found himself straining to hear a melody in the creaks and groans, wondering if somewhere, in a room they hadn't found yet, a piano was waiting to be played again.

* * *

Wesley pushed the shopping cart down the aisle, its squeaky wheel providing an oddly comforting rhythm. Normal. Mundane. Everything the past few days hadn't been. He grabbed essentials mechanically: bread, milk, eggs; anchors of ordinary life that felt increasingly distant from whatever was happening at the Hawthorne Estate.

He paused in front of the cereal section, reaching for Teddy's favorite. The bright cartoon character on the box seemed to mock him with its cheerfulness. How long had it been since Teddy had eaten a proper breakfast? Since he'd done anything but drift between strange conversations and exhausted sleep? It may have been less than a week, but it also felt like an age.

"Oh, excuse me, dear."

Wesley startled, nearly dropping the cereal box as an elderly woman maneuvered her cart around his. She paused, studying his face with surprising intensity.

"You look like you're carrying the weight of the world on your shoulders," she said, her voice gentle. "New parent?"

Wesley managed a weak smile. "No, just... dealing with a sick kid. Family friend's son."

"Ah," she nodded sagely. "Nothing worse than seeing a child unwell. Have you tried-"

"Honey and lemon tea? Vitamin C? Essential oils?" Wesley rattled off Charlie's growing list of attempted remedies.

The woman laughed. "I was going to suggest a good night's sleep, but it seems you've got plenty of advice already."

If only it were that simple, Wesley thought as he finished his shopping. Regular medicine, regular advice; none of it seemed to apply to whatever was happening to Teddy.

When he pulled into the driveway, he spotted a pile of packages on the porch. More of Charlie's attempts to find answers, no doubt. He gathered the grocery bags and made his way up the steps, noting the various shipping labels. Some were from normal pharmacies, others from websites he'd never heard of: "Mystic Meadows Healing," "The Crystal Cottage," "Ancient Wisdom Imports."

The moment Wesley opened the front door, he was hit by an overwhelming herbal smell; something between his grandmother's vegetable soup and a bread shop. He blinked, taking in the bizarre sight before him. About a dozen small potted plants lined the walls of the foyer, their silvery-green leaves unmistakable.

"Charlie?" Wesley called out, completely baffled. "Why does my house look like a garden center?"

He found Charlie in the living room, his laptop balanced precariously on the arm of the couch while Teddy dozed fitfully beside him. A thin tendril of smoke curled up from the fireplace, where the charred remains of what looked like small branches still smoldered.

"Please tell me you didn't try to start a forest fire in my living room," Wesley said, setting down the groceries.

Charlie had the grace to look slightly sheepish. "It's sage," he muttered, not quite meeting Wesley's eyes.

"Sage," Wesley repeated flatly. "And you needed... twelve plants worth?"

"The forums said you're supposed to burn it in every room," Charlie explained, as if this was perfectly reasonable. "But then I read that living plants have more power, so..." he gestured vaguely at the impromptu indoor garden.

Wesley pinched the bridge of his nose. "And the overwhelming smell?"

Charlie glanced at the fireplace. "I might have gotten a little enthusiastic with the burning part. Did you know sage bundles are actually pretty flammable?"

"No, Charlie, I did not know that. Just like I didn't know my house would end up smelling like an Italian restaurant having an identity crisis."

"The lady at The Crystal Cottage said the smell means it's

working," Charlie said defensively.

Wesley looked at the packages by the door. "Please tell me you didn't buy more sage."

Charlie's silence was answer enough.

Wesley set the groceries down and went to retrieve the packages. When he returned, Charlie was already opening the first box, revealing an assortment of herbs and crystals.

"This one's supposed to promote restful sleep," Charlie explained, holding up a small purple crystal. "And these herbs... well, the website said they're traditionally used for protection against negative energies."

Wesley picked up a small cloth bag filled with what looked like dried flowers. "Protection against what, exactly?"

"At this point?" Charlie glanced at Teddy's sleeping form. "Whatever's making my son fade away in front of my eyes."

The weight of those words hung in the air between them, making the house's silence feel heavier than ever.

* * *

Wesley reorganized another shelf in his study, trying to lose himself in the mundane task of alphabetizing books. The television droned from the living room, some cheerful cartoon Charlie had put on in hopes of keeping Teddy awake for more than an hour at a time.

The sound of breaking glass shattered the artificial calm.

Wesley's heart leaped into his throat as Teddy's scream echoed through the house. He dropped the book he was holding, barely registering the thud as it hit the floor. By the time he reached the living room, Charlie was already there, kneeling beside Teddy who was thrashing on the floor.

The boy's movements were wrong; not like a seizure, but like someone fighting against a current. His hands clawed at the air, his legs kicking against nothing, while his eyes... his eyes stared at something neither man could see.

"Teddy!" Charlie's voice cracked as he tried to hold his son still. "Buddy, please!"

"The water!" Teddy gasped between screams. "The water's too deep!"

Wesley fell to his knees beside them, his mind racing. "Charlie, we need to-"

"Hospital," Charlie nodded, already gathering Teddy into his arms. "Now."

They rushed toward the front door, Charlie cradling Teddy while Wesley grabbed car keys with shaking hands. But as Charlie crossed the threshold, something impossible happened.

Teddy's legs began to fade, becoming transparent like morning mist. Charlie stumbled backward in horror, and the moment they were fully inside again, Teddy became solid once more.

"No," Charlie whispered, his face ashen. "No, no, no..."

Wesley watched, paralyzed, as Charlie tried again. This time, Teddy's whole lower body started to disappear the moment it passed the doorway. Charlie jerked back inside, clutching his son closer.

"She won't let me leave," Teddy whimpered, his voice small and frightened. "She says I have to stay until I remember."

"Remember what?" Wesley asked, his own voice barely a whisper.

But Teddy had already slipped into unconsciousness, his body limp in Charlie's arms. The house creaked around them, a sound that seemed almost satisfied.

Charlie looked at Wesley, his eyes wild with fear and helpless rage. "What do we do now?"

Wesley stared at the open doorway; such a simple thing, a rectangle of late afternoon light that had somehow become an impossible barrier. They couldn't leave, couldn't get help. Whatever was happening to Teddy, whatever force had taken hold of him, it had them all trapped now.

"We find answers," Wesley said, his voice steadier than he felt. "Whatever this house is hiding, whatever Evelyn wants Teddy to remember, we find it. Before it's too late."

4

Wesley stood watching Charlie cradle Teddy on the floor for a moment, the impossible scene of his godson's partial disappearance replaying in his mind. The house seemed to hold its breath around them, the usual creaks and settling sounds conspicuously absent. Even the old grandfather clock in the hall had fallen silent, though Wesley could have sworn it had been ticking moments ago.

"The lady wanted me to stay," Teddy mumbled against Charlie's chest, his voice small but steady. "She says I have to help her remember."

Charlie's arms tightened around his son. "Remember what, buddy?"

"I don't know." Teddy's eyes drooped, his small fingers clutching his father's shirt. "She keeps showing me the lake, but everything's dark and cold... and someone's crying."

Wesley felt his blood run cold at the mention of the lake

68

again. He knelt beside them, noting how Teddy's skin felt like ice despite the warm summer evening. Charlie looked up at him, fear warring with determination in his eyes.

"Like you said, we need answers," Charlie said, his voice rough. "Real ones. Not forum theories or..." he glanced at the pile of spiritual remedies in the corner, a mix of embarrassment and frustration crossing his face, "whatever all that was supposed to be."

"The census records came in," Wesley said, already mentally cataloging their resources. "And there's that letter I never opened; the one with the fancy seal."

"Then that's where we start," Charlie said, shifting Teddy in his arms as he stood. "No more random attempts. We do this right."

The house creaked then, a long, low sound like a sigh. Or perhaps, Wesley thought, like agreement.

"Can you walk, buddy?" Charlie asked softly, but Teddy had already drifted off to sleep, his face peaceful for the first time in hours.

Wesley helped Charlie carry Teddy upstairs to his bedroom. They moved carefully, both hyper-aware of the doorways they passed through, though nothing strange happened this time. The boy didn't stir as Charlie laid him on his bed, didn't wake when Wesley pulled the blanket up to his chin.

"I'll stay with him," Charlie said, settling into the chair beside the bed. "You start on those records."

Wesley nodded, turning to leave, but paused at the doorway. "Charlie?"

"Yeah?"

"We're going to figure this out." He tried to inject more confidence into his voice than he felt. "Whatever's happening here, whatever this Evelyn wants..."

"I know," Charlie said quietly, his eyes never leaving Teddy's face. "We don't have a choice anymore."

The house creaked again as Wesley headed downstairs, its sounds somehow more purposeful than before. Or maybe he was just finally starting to listen properly. Either way, the time for half-measures and wild guesses was over.

Wesley paused in the hallway, his hand trailing along the wall. The house felt different now, as if their acknowledgment of its mysteries had changed something fundamental about the space they occupied. Even the shadows seemed deeper.

He gathered the scattered research materials from the living room: printouts from paranormal forums, Charlie's collection of protective herbs, the hastily scrawled notes about the house's history. Each item represented a desperate attempt to understand what was happening. Some of those attempts, he realized now, might not have been as misguided as they'd seemed.

The protection herbs Charlie had burned actually had seemed to help Teddy sleep. The salt lines, ridiculous as they'd appeared, had given them a sense of control when they'd had none. Even the failed rituals had led them here, to this moment of clarity.

Wesley organized everything into neat piles, trying to impose order on chaos. One stack for property record printouts, another for local legends, a third for the various supernatural theories they'd collected. Somewhere in this mess of information lay the truth about the Hawthorne Estate, about Evelyn, about why she'd chosen Teddy.

A floorboard creaked behind him, and Wesley turned, half-expecting to see a ghostly figure. Instead, he found only moonlight streaming through the window, casting strange patterns on the floor. For a moment, the shadows looked like ripples on water.

It was time to figure out the truth, no matter how impossible it might seem.

* * *

Wesley's eyes felt like sandpaper as he stared at his laptop screen, the harsh glare of the kitchen lights making the census records blur together. Coffee cups littered the table around him, a timeline of his growing frustration marked in caffeine rings and scattered sugar packets.

The census records were comprehensive, almost overwhelmingly so. Generations of Hawthornes had lived in the estate, their lives documented in neat columns of dates and names. Wesley had created a makeshift family tree on a word document, trying to track the relationships and connections that might lead them to answers.

His eyes caught on a name, but not the one he'd been expecting. "Look at this," he called to Charlie, who was poring over their copy of downloaded property records across the table. "There's a note about a ward taken in by the Hawthornes in 1889. Evelyn Hartley."

Charlie's head snapped up. "Evelyn? Like..."

"Like Teddy's invisible friend," Wesley finished. He

clicked through several more documents, his heart racing. "She would have been about seventeen in 1895, right around when the property records show major changes to the estate grounds."

"What kind of changes?"

Wesley pulled up the relevant documents. "The lake. That's when they filled in the lake." He scrolled through the records, his frown deepening. "But look at the timing. The lake was filled in February 1895, right after..." He trailed off, a chill running down his spine.

"Right after what?" Charlie leaned forward, his own research forgotten.

"Right after Evelyn's death." Wesley's voice was barely a whisper. "There's a death certificate here. She died of exposure and drowning in January 1895."

The lights flickered overhead, making both men jump. From upstairs came the sound of Teddy's voice, too faint to make out the words but carrying that same sing-song quality it had when he spoke to his invisible friend.

Charlie was already halfway to the stairs when Wesley caught his arm. "Wait. There's more." He clicked on the link to an old newspaper clipping. "Evelyn wasn't alone that day. She was with her cousins, probably the Hawthorne children. Alaric and Joseph."

"What happened to them?"

Before Wesley could answer, a crash echoed from upstairs, followed by Teddy's frightened cry. They both bolted for the stairs, taking them two at a time. The temperature dropped noticeably as they reached the second floor, their breath visible in the suddenly frigid air.

They found Teddy sitting up in bed, staring at his window where frost patterns were spreading across the glass despite the summer heat outside. The patterns weren't random: they formed words, written in a delicate, feminine hand:

"Help me find him."

The writing began to fade almost immediately as the frost melted, but Wesley had already pulled out his phone, snapping several quick photos. They had more proof now; real, tangible evidence that something supernatural was happening. But more importantly, they had a clue about what Evelyn wanted.

She was still looking for that 'Larry' person. Alaric? And somehow, Teddy was the key to helping her find him.

Charlie carefully wiped the frost from the window, his hands shaking slightly. "Look at this," he said softly.

Beneath the written message, the frost had formed another pattern; the delicate outline of a child's hand, pressed against the glass from the other side. As they watched, a second, larger handprint appeared beside it, as if someone was reaching out to hold the child's hand.

Teddy stirred in his bed. "She used to hold his hand when he was scared," he mumbled, still half-asleep. "When the thunder was too loud, or the dark was too dark."

Wesley quickly took pictures of the handprints before they could fade. The temperature in the room slowly began to normalize, but the sense of presence remained; a watchful, waiting energy that made the hair on the back of his neck stand up.

"We should check the attic," Charlie said suddenly. "Old

houses like this, people always stored things in attics. Family records, photographs..."

"Memories, though I'm unsure if they'd still be there; family probably would've collected them long ago," Wesley agreed. He looked at his phone, at the mysterious handprints captured in digital clarity. "Tomorrow morning, first thing. Whatever Evelyn's trying to tell us, we're running out of time to hear it."

The frost melted completely, leaving the window clear and ordinary once more. But Wesley couldn't shake the image of those handprints; one small and uncertain, the other protective and sure. Like Evelyn and Alaric. Like Charlie and Teddy.

Some patterns, it seemed, echoed across time.

* * *

Wesley's fingers flew across the keyboard, his search terms now focused and deliberate. The local newspaper's digital archive was a maze of poorly scanned documents and broken links, but he refused to give up. Not when they were finally getting somewhere.

"Here," he said suddenly, turning his laptop so Charlie could see. "January 15th, 1895. 'Tragedy at Hawthorne Estate.'"

Charlie leaned in, his eyes scanning the faded text. The article was brief but devastating in its simplicity: two children on the ice, one falling through, a brave young woman diving in to save them. Only one name was mentioned directly: Evelyn Hartley, age 17, who succumbed to the cold before help could arrive.

"They didn't name the children," Wesley muttered, scrolling through the article again. "Privacy concerns, probably. But look at this line: 'The Hawthorne family requests privacy in their time of mourning.'"

"Mourning," Charlie repeated, his face pale. "Does that mean..."

Wesley was already pulling up the next week's edition. His breath caught as he found another article, this one even shorter. "Found him. Alaric Hawthorne, age 4." He swallowed hard. "They recovered his body when the weather warmed enough to break up the ice."

The lights flickered overhead, and a cold breeze swept through the kitchen despite the closed windows. Charlie shivered, wrapping his arms around himself.

"She never knew," Wesley said softly. "Evelyn died not knowing if she'd saved him."

"And now she's looking for him?" Charlie's voice was hoarse. "After all this time?"

"Not looking," Wesley corrected, the pieces finally falling into place. "Remembering. She wants to remember what happened that day. And somehow..." He trailed off, his eyes widening in sudden understanding.

"Somehow what?"

"Teddy. He's the same age Alaric was." Wesley's heart was pounding now. "That's why she's drawn to him. Why she's showing him the lake, the music room..."

Charlie's face hardened. "She's not using my son as some kind of supernatural surrogate."

As if in response to his words, a series of thuds echoed

from upstairs; the same rhythm they'd heard before, like someone pacing back and forth. But this time, it was accompanied by the faint sound of piano music, so distant it might have been imagination.

They found Teddy in the hallway, standing in his pajamas, staring at nothing. No, not nothing. He was watching something they couldn't see, his eyes tracking movement that wasn't there.

"She's crying again," Teddy said quietly. "She couldn't find him in the dark water."

The temperature around them plummeted, and Wesley's phone chimed with a notification. The local historical society had responded to his earlier inquiry:

"Recently digitized photos from 1895 attached. Warning: some content may be disturbing."

Charlie reached for his phone, then hesitated. "I should check on Teddy first."

"He's still in the hallway," Wesley said, not looking up from his screen. "Hasn't moved."

"How do you-" Charlie stopped as Wesley pointed to the window. Their reflections were clear in the dark glass, and behind them, Teddy's small figure was visible in the hallway mirror. The boy stood perfectly still, as if listening to something only he could hear.

Another notification pinged on Wesley's phone, a second email from the historical society:

"Additional note: Found reference to piano sheet music in estate inventory. Piece titled 'Remember the Lake' by E. Hartley, never published. Original manuscript missing."

"She was a composer?" Charlie asked, reading over Wesley's shoulder.

"Or trying to be." Wesley opened a new search tab. "Look at this: there are mentions in the society pages about musical evenings at the estate. Evelyn would play while the children danced."

The house creaked, a long, low sound that might have been appreciation. Wesley thought he heard a faint melody threaded through the usual settling noises, but it was gone before he could be sure.

"The piano was her connection," he said slowly. "To the house, to the children, to... everything." He looked at Charlie. "That's why Teddy keeps hearing music. She's trying to share her memories the only way she knows how."

From the hallway, Teddy's voice drifted down: "She says the music helps her remember. But sometimes remembering hurts too much."

* * *

Charlie worked methodically, his movements precise despite his exhaustion. Wesley watched from the doorway as his friend hung another small mirror, this one angled to catch the morning light just so.

"The forums said mirrors can trap negative energy," Charlie explained before Wesley could ask. He gestured to the line of salt tracing the doorway, the bundles of dried herbs hanging from the curtain rods. "And the herbs are supposed to promote peaceful sleep."

"Charlie..."

"I know how it looks," Charlie interrupted, adjusting the mirror slightly. "But the salt actually seems to help. Teddy sleeps better with it at the doors." He paused, his hand resting on the frame. "And if there's even a chance it's protecting him..."

Wesley stepped into the room, taking in the careful arrangements. The mirrors were placed strategically, creating a web of reflected light that somehow made the room feel warmer, safer. The herbs filled the air with a subtle, soothing scent that reminded him of his grandmother's garden.

"Besides," Charlie added quietly, "it makes me feel like I'm doing something. Like I'm not completely helpless while my son..." He trailed off, his hands tightening on the mirror he held until his knuckles went white.

Wesley stepped forward and took the mirror, helping to hang it. Sometimes protection came in strange forms, and who was he to judge what gave his friend comfort?

"Did you know," Charlie said, reaching for another mirror, "that in some cultures, they believe mirrors can show the truth of things? Not just reflections, but what's really there."

Wesley glanced at their reflections, multiplied across the room's surfaces. For a moment, he thought he saw something else: a flash of dark hair, a pale face; but it was gone before he could be sure.

"I've been thinking," Charlie continued, his voice steady despite the tremor in his hands. "Maybe we've been looking at this wrong. Maybe Evelyn isn't trying to hurt Teddy. Maybe she's trying to protect him from whatever happened to her cousin."

"By trapping him here?"

"By keeping him away from the water." Charlie met Wesley's eyes in one of the mirrors. "You saw those articles. A four year old boy, falling through the ice. Evelyn diving in after him. What if she's not trying to make Teddy remember; what if she's trying to prevent history from repeating itself?"

Before Wesley could respond, Teddy stirred in his sleep. The boy's face scrunched up, his hands clutching at his blanket. "Cold," he mumbled. "The water's so cold..."

Charlie was there in an instant, smoothing Teddy's hair back from his forehead. "It's okay, buddy. You're safe. You're warm and dry and safe."

The mirrors caught the morning light, sending it dancing across the walls like ripples on water. Wesley watched as Teddy settled, his face relaxing under his father's touch. The protection might not be perfect, might not even be real in any tangible sense. But right now, in this room full of reflected light and father's love, it felt like enough.

At least until they could find the truth in those historical society photos and finally understand what Evelyn was trying to tell them.

Wesley helped Charlie hang the last mirror then stepped back to survey their work. The morning light created an intricate dance of reflections.

Charlie sighed. "The forums said mirrors are like doorways sometimes. Between here and... wherever 'there' is." He adjusted one slightly, changing the pattern of light. "I thought it was nonsense at first, but now..."

"Now nothing seems impossible," Wesley finished. He watched the light play across the walls, remembering the frost patterns on the window, the mysterious handprints that had appeared and vanished.

Teddy stirred again in his sleep, but this time his face was peaceful. The protection, whether from the mirrors, the salt, the herbs, or simply his father's presence, seemed to be working. For now.

Charlie sat on the edge of the bed, gently smoothing Teddy's hair back from his forehead. "You know what's strange?" he said quietly. "When I was hanging these mirrors, I could have sworn I saw... not a ghost, exactly. More like memories. Children playing, a girl at a piano."

"I guess the house really remembers," Wesley said, surprising himself with the certainty in his voice. "And maybe, through Teddy, it's trying to help Evelyn remember too."

The morning light shifted, sending one beam directly onto Teddy's face. The boy smiled in his sleep, as if dreaming of something pleasant. For the first time in days, he looked like himself again; not a conduit for century-old grief, but simply a sleeping child, safe in his father's care.

* * *

Wesley's hands shook slightly as he downloaded the attachments from the historical society. Each image seemed to load with agonizing slowness. Charlie leaned over his shoulder, both men holding their breath.

The first few photos were typical Victorian family portraits. Stiff poses, serious faces, elaborate clothing. But

Wesley's attention caught on one face that appeared repeatedly: a young woman with dark hair and pale features, her expression somehow softer than the others despite the formal setting.

"That's her, isn't it?" Charlie whispered. "Evelyn."

Wesley nodded, unable to speak. In each photo, Evelyn stood near two small boys, her protective stance obvious even through the century-old images. One boy, the younger one, smiled readily at the camera. The other, Alaric, Wesley realized with a jolt, seemed more reserved, always turning slightly toward Evelyn as if seeking reassurance.

The next photo made both men catch their breath. It showed the estate's grounds in winter, the lake stretching out behind the house like a mirror. Children played on the frozen surface while adults watched from the shore. The date on the photo: January 12th, 1895, just days before the tragedy.

"Look," Wesley said, zooming in on a detail in the background. "The music room window. You can see the piano."

Indeed, through the large bay window, a grand piano was barely visible in the grainy image. But what caught Wesley's attention was a figure seated at it; likely Evelyn again, suggesting she was playing while watching the children outside.

The final photo stopped his heart. Unlike the others, this one wasn't formal or staged. It showed Evelyn outdoors, caught in a rare moment of laughter as she played with the boys in the estate's garden. Someone had written on the back in flowing script: "Evelyn with Alaric and Joseph, Summer 1894. The last happy summer."

"She loved them," Charlie said softly. "Those boys weren't just her cousins; she was like a mother to them."

"And she died trying to save them." Wesley's voice cracked. He looked at the date again, his mind racing. "Like we said earlier Charlie, what if that's why she's here? Why she's drawn to Teddy? He's not only the same age as Alaric, he's the same kind of child. Bright, curious..."

"Protected," Charlie finished, sagging in his chair. "She's truly been trying to protect him all along."

The lights flickered, and Wesley's laptop screen went black. Before either man could react, it came back on, cycling through the photos rapidly before stopping on one they hadn't seen before. The image showed the music room again, but this time Evelyn sat at the piano with Alaric beside her, his small hands positioned over the keys as she taught him to play.

The image began to change, colors bleeding into the black and white photograph as if someone was painting it in real time. The pale blue of Alaric's jacket, the deep burgundy of Evelyn's dress, the warm wood tones of the piano; they all emerged with perfect clarity.

And then, impossibly, the photo began to move. Just slightly, just for a moment; Evelyn's hands guided Alaric's over the keys, both smiling as music only they could hear played.

The laptop slammed shut by itself, plunging them into silence.

From upstairs, clear as a bell, came the sound of piano music shortly after.

But it wasn't just music: it was a specific piece, one that

made Charlie's head snap up in recognition.

"That's the lullaby," he whispered. "The one Teddy's been humming in his sleep."

Wesley felt a chill run down his spine. He reopened his laptop to click back through the photos, looking more carefully at the piano in each shot. There, just visible on the music stand in one image: handwritten sheet music, the title partially visible - "Remember the..."

"She wrote it for them," he realized. "For Alaric and Joseph. A lullaby to help them sleep, to chase away bad dreams." He zoomed in on Evelyn's face in the last photo, seeing now what he'd missed before; bone-deep protectiveness. The same look he'd seen on Charlie's face these past few days.

The laptop screen flickered again, and new text appeared in an open document:

"The music helps them sleep. Keeps the dark away. But that day, the ice called louder than my song."

Charlie's breath caught. "Is she..."

"Writing to us? I think so." Wesley's fingers hovered over the keyboard. "Should I respond?"

Before he could decide, more text appeared:

"He needs to understand. They both do. Please."

The piano music grew louder, more insistent. It was a call, a plea, a bridge between past and present.

"Both?" Charlie asked, his voice tight with worry.

Wesley looked at him. "Teddy... and you. A child in

danger and the one who loves him most. She's trying to show you something, too."

* * *

They took the stairs two at a time, following the haunting melody that seemed to come from everywhere and nowhere at once. The air grew colder with each step, their breath visible in the suddenly frigid hallway.

They found Teddy standing in front of a wall where there had never been a door before. But now an ornate frame had emerged from the paneling, its wood darker and older than the surrounding walls. Through the gap, they could see a room that couldn't exist: the music room from the photographs, perfectly preserved.

A grand piano dominated the space, its keys moving by themselves as the melody continued. Teddy swayed slightly, as if dancing to the music.

"She taught him this song," Teddy said, his voice distant. "Every evening before bed. But that day... that day he wanted to see something on the ice instead."

"Teddy," Charlie called, his voice tight with fear. "Teddy, come away from there."

But Teddy took a step forward, his hand reaching for the doorknob. "She needs to remember. She needs to know..."

"No!" Charlie lunged forward, but the temperature dropped so suddenly it stole his breath. Ice crystals formed on the walls, spreading in delicate patterns that spelled out words:

"Please. He needs to see."

Wesley caught Charlie's arm. "Wait," he said, though every instinct screamed at him to grab Teddy and run. "I think... I think we need to let this happen."

"Are you insane?" Charlie's voice cracked. "That room doesn't exist! None of this is real!"

"But it was," Wesley said softly. "Once. And maybe that's what Evelyn's been trying to tell us all along. She's not trying to take Teddy; I think she's trying to show him something. Something she needs to remember herself."

The piano music swelled, and Teddy stepped through the doorway. This time, he didn't fade or disappear. Instead, he seemed to glow slightly, as if lit from within. He walked to the piano, his movements dreamlike.

A figure shimmered into existence beside him, a young woman with dark hair and a pale face, her form translucent but undeniably real. Evelyn.

She smiled down at Teddy, then looked up at Charlie and Wesley. Her lips moved, forming words they could almost hear: "I'll keep him safe. I promise."

And then the world around them began to change.

The transformation wasn't merely visual; it was complete, overwhelming, as if reality itself had become fluid. Wesley felt a strange doubling of his senses; the present and the past seemed to overlap, each equally real and unreal.

The air filled with the scents of another time: beeswax candles, leather-bound books, the peculiar mustiness of Victorian furnishings. Even the light changed, becoming softer, filtered through glass that had been hand-blown a century ago.

Charlie reached for Teddy instinctively, but his hand passed through his son as if through mist. "Wes?" His voice shook slightly.

"I don't think we can interfere," Wesley said, though the words felt hollow in his mouth. "This is... I think this is what she's been trying to show us all along. The whole truth."

Teddy stood by the piano, but he wasn't quite Teddy anymore. His modern pajamas had been replaced by Victorian children's clothes, his posture subtly different. When he turned to look at them, his eyes held an old soul's wisdom.

"She needs you to understand," he said, his voice a strange blend of Teddy's childish tones and something older, more formal. "About love. About sacrifice. About choices made in moments when there are no good choices left."

Evelyn's form solidified further, her ghostly hands poised over the piano keys. The melody she played was the lullaby, but underneath it ran another theme; it was darker, sadder, like ice cracking over deep water.

"Remember," she whispered, her voice carrying despite its softness. "Remember with me."

The walls began to blur, the familiar lines of the house dissolving into something else entirely. They were about to see what really happened that winter day: the truth that had been buried with the lake.

* * *

The music room continued to dissolve around them like watercolor in rain, reforming into a winter landscape. The lake stretched before them, its surface a patchwork of snow and ice. The cold felt real, but when Wesley reached out to touch a nearby tree, his hand passed through it.

"We're in her memory," he whispered.

They watched as three figures approached the lake: Evelyn, tall and graceful in her dark wool coat, and two small boys similarly bundled against the cold. The younger one, Joseph, danced ahead while Alaric stayed close to Evelyn's side.

"Look!" Memory-Alaric pointed toward the center of the lake. "There is something shining out there!"

Memory-Evelyn squinted against the glare. "It is probably just ice, Larry. We should head back; it is nearly time for your piano lesson."

But Alaric was already edging onto the ice, his curiosity overtaking his usual caution. "I just want to see what it is. Please, Evelyn?"

Present-day Teddy moved toward them, his eyes fixed on Alaric. They were mirror images of each other: same age, same wonder-filled expression. Charlie made an aborted movement to stop him, but Wesley caught his arm.

"We can't change what happened," Wesley said softly. "This is just a memory."

They watched as Memory-Evelyn carefully followed Alaric onto the ice, testing each step. Joseph remained on the shore, calling out encouragement to his brother. The surface seemed solid enough at first, but then-

A crack. A splash. A scream.

Alaric disappeared beneath the dark water. Without hesitation, Memory-Evelyn dove in after him. Joseph's terrified cries echoed across the lake as he ran for help.

The scene blurred, time speeding up. People arrived with ropes and poles, dragging through the lake. They pulled Evelyn out first, her lips blue, her dark hair frozen in tendrils around her face. She was barely breathing when they carried her toward the house.

"Please," she whispered, her voice carrying across time. "Please, you have to find him. Alaric... where is Alaric?"

But she never heard the answer. Her eyes closed, her breath stilled, and Evelyn Hartley slipped away.

The scene faded, bringing them back to the present-day music room. Teddy stood by the piano, tears rolling down his cheeks. The ghostly figure of Evelyn materialized beside him; her own face wet with phantom tears.

"Now you know," Teddy said, but his voice had changed - deeper, older somehow. "Now you remember."

Evelyn nodded, reaching out as if to touch his cheek but stopping just short. "I tried so hard to reach him," she whispered, her voice like wind through leaves. "The water was so dark, so cold. I could hear him calling for me, but I could not..."

"It was not your fault," Teddy said. No, not Teddy, Wesley realized. For just a moment, another boy seemed

to shine through him, like light through stained glass.

Alaric.

The air shimmered around them, and for a moment they could see both scenes superimposed: the frozen lake of 1895 and the present-day room, like double-exposed photographs. In both times, a child stood at the edge of danger while someone who loved them watched helplessly.

"I remember now," Teddy said, but his voice seemed to come from far away. "The watch was so pretty in the sunlight. Like a star fallen on the ice."

Charlie made another aborted movement toward his son, his parental instincts warring with the impossibility of the situation. Wesley caught his arm again, but this time in support rather than restraint.

"Look," Wesley whispered, pointing to where the memory-scene continued to play out.

They could see it more clearly now - the pocket watch lying on the ice, its gold case catching the winter sun. Memory-Alaric's face lit up with childish delight at the discovery. But there was something else, something they hadn't noticed before.

There was a pattern to the cracks in the ice where Alaric had fallen through, as if...

"Someone broke it," Charlie breathed, horror dawning in his voice. "Probably the night before. Someone walked out there and deliberately weakened the ice."

Memory-Evelyn's voice drifted across time: "Robert, please, the ice is not safe yet!"

But her uncle, standing at the edge of the lake, merely shook his head. "Nonsense, girl. Winter has been cold enough. The boys need their exercise."

The present-day Evelyn flickered like a candle flame, her form becoming more solid as the truth emerged. Her face held a century of unspoken words, of accusations never made, of suspicions buried with her in that frozen grave.

"He knew," she whispered, her voice like wind through bare branches. "He knew the ice was weak, but he let them play there anyway. His own sons..." She looked at Teddy, and for a moment they could see Alaric shining through him even more clearly. "I could not save him then. But I can protect now. I can remember."

The memory rippled, showing them one final detail they'd missed: Robert Hawthorne standing on the shore, watching the tragedy unfold, making no move to help as his niece dove into the freezing water to save his son.

* * *

The revelation hit Wesley like a physical blow.

Evelyn turned to him, her form becoming clearer. "I have been trapped here for so long," she said. "Watching families come and go, trying to remember what happened that day. But the memories were too painful, too fragmented." She smiled sadly at Teddy. "Until he came. His light, his innocence... it reminded me so much of Alaric."

"But the lake," Charlie said, stepping forward. His protective instincts warred with understanding on his face. "The messages, keeping Teddy here..."

"I had to know," Evelyn whispered. "Had to remember. And once I started remembering, I could not let him near water, near danger. I could not fail another child."

Teddy blinked, and he was fully himself again. He swayed slightly, and Charlie rushed forward to catch him.

"Daddy?" Teddy looked up, confused. "I saw... I remember..."

"Shh, buddy. I've got you." Charlie cradled his son close.

Wesley turned to Evelyn, whose form was beginning to fade. "Alaric...?"

"Yes," she said softly. "When the ice melted. He was..." she paused, a century of grief in her eyes. "He was holding the thing that had caught his attention. A pocket watch, dropped by a skater the day before. He had just wanted to return it."

The piano played a single, soft note. Evelyn turned toward it, a real smile crossing her face for the first time. "He loved music so much," she said. "We were supposed to practice that evening. I had promised to teach him a new song."

"That's why the music room appears," Wesley realized. "It's a promise unfulfilled."

Evelyn nodded. "I have been holding on to so much. The guilt, the fear, the not knowing... but now..." She looked at Teddy with infinite tenderness. "Now I remember everything. Even the good parts. Especially the good parts."

The room began to fade around them, the grand piano becoming transparent. Evelyn's form flickered like a candle flame.

"Thank you," she said to Teddy. "For helping me remember. For letting me protect someone one last time."

"Will you go away now?" Teddy asked, his voice small.

"No, dear heart. But I will not need to hold on so tightly anymore." She smiled at Charlie. "He is safe with you. Just as Alaric was loved by me."

The music room dissolved completely, leaving them in the normal upstairs hallway. The door had vanished as if it had never been there. But a warmth lingered in the air, and somewhere in the distance, they could hear the faint notes of a piano playing a lullaby.

Wesley looked at Charlie, both men processing the weight of what they'd witnessed. They had their answers now: about the lake, about Evelyn, about why she'd been drawn to Teddy. But more importantly, they understood what needed to be done.

It was time to help both the living and the dead find peace.

The warmth that lingered in the air took on a different quality now; less like remembered sunshine and more like a gentle embrace. Teddy swayed on his feet, suddenly fully himself again, and Charlie gathered him close.

"Is she still here?" Teddy asked sleepily, his head heavy on his father's shoulder.

As if in answer, the temperature shifted slightly, and the scent of piano polish and lavender drifted through the air; Evelyn's signature perfume, they now knew, from the memories they'd witnessed.

"I guess she'll always be here," Wesley said, understanding at last. "But not as a ghost trapped between moments. Not anymore."

Charlie looked around the hallway, his eyes catching on the mirrors he'd hung in Teddy's room. Each one reflected a slightly different scene now: children playing, a young woman at a piano, moments of joy preserved like insects in amber.

"The house really remembers," Charlie said softly, echoing Wesley's earlier words. "That's what all this was about, wasn't it? Every moment of love, every song, every..." he swallowed hard, "every sacrifice."

Wesley nodded, his mind already turning to what needed to be done next. The truth about Robert Hawthorne's role in the tragedy had been buried along with the lake, but perhaps that truth deserved to be remembered too. To honor Evelyn and what she'd lost.

"Tomorrow," he said, "we start looking for that music manuscript. The one Evelyn wrote." He glanced at Teddy, now sleeping peacefully in Charlie's arms. "I think... I think that's what she wants us to find next. Not the lullaby; what she wrote after. When she knew what was going to happen."

The house creaked its agreement, the sound somehow both ending and beginning. They had uncovered one truth, but another waited to be found. The next chapter would bring its own challenges, its own revelations.

But for now, in this moment between knowledge and action, they stood together in the hallway of a house that remembered everything.

5

The morning light filtered through the windows, casting a dull glow over the Hawthorne Estate. The air was thick with an almost palpable tension, a heaviness that seemed to press down on Wesley as he stirred from his fitful sleep. The house felt different; darker, colder. He could see his breath misting in the frigid air, the temperature having dropped significantly overnight.

Wesley swung his legs over the side of the bed, his feet meeting the cold floor with a jolt. He wrapped a blanket around his shoulders and stepped out into the hallway. The chill was pervasive, seeping into his bones. He glanced at the thermostat, noting that it read a full ten degrees lower than he'd set it the night before.

Wesley's mind tried to rationalize the dropping temperature, mentally calculating how long it would take pipes to freeze, and how quickly frost could naturally form. But there was nothing natural about the way the ice crystals spread across the windows, forming and reforming into words with deliberate precision.

"The thermostat's dead," Charlie called from downstairs, his attempt at normalcy almost comical in its futility. "Though I guess ghost-induced freezing probably isn't covered under the warranty."

The weak joke fell flat as another message etched itself into the frost: "Keep him safe." The letters formed with the careful deliberation of someone who had spent years teaching children their penmanship.

Wesley touched the glass, expecting the frost to melt under his fingertip. Instead, the ice grew thicker, spreading outward from his touch like ripples in a pond. The message changed, becoming more urgent: "He must not leave. He must not freeze. Not like-"

The final words were lost as the entire window frosted over.

Wesley's heart pounded in his chest as he hurried down to the kitchen. The house felt alive with an energy that was both protective and suffocating. He found Charlie already there, his face pale and his eyes wide with worry.

"Wes," Charlie said, his voice barely above a whisper. "The doors... they're sealed."

Wesley's gaze flicked to the back door, where a thick layer of ice coated the handle and the frame. He moved to the front door, finding it similarly encased. Panic began to rise in his throat, but he swallowed it down, focusing on what needed to be done.

"Teddy!" Wesley and Charlie said in unison; Wesley's steady voice clashing with the panicked tone of Charlie's.

They scrambled up the stairs together, the air growing colder with each step. When they reached Teddy's room, they found the boy huddled under his blankets, his face pale and his breathing shallow. Charlie rushed to his side, gently shaking him awake.

"Teddy," Charlie called, his voice laced with fear. "Buddy, wake up."

Teddy's eyes fluttered open, but they were glassy and unfocused. He looked up at his father, a weak smile playing on his lips. "Daddy," he murmured, his voice barely audible.

Wesley's heart sank as he watched Teddy struggle to stay awake. Evelyn's presence was stronger than ever. Despite their seemingly amicable parting the previous day, it seemed like the knowledge of her uncle's betrayal had intensified her fear for Teddy and the house was responding to her emotions.

Charlie lifted Teddy into his arms, cradling him close. "We need to get him warm," he said, his voice trembling slightly.

Wesley nodded, his mind racing. They needed to find a way to break through the ice, to escape the house's grip. But first, they needed to take care of Teddy. As they made their way back downstairs, Wesley couldn't shake the feeling that they were being watched, that Evelyn's spirit was hovering nearby, her fear and desperation palpable.

The house creaked and groaned around them, the sound ominous and foreboding. Wesley's gaze flicked to the windows, where the frost continued to spread, the messages becoming more urgent, more insistent. They were cut off from the outside world, at the mercy of a spirit whose love and fear had turned into something dark and dangerous.

As they settled Teddy onto the sofa, wrapping him in blankets and trying to warm him up, Wesley couldn't help but wonder what Evelyn wanted from them. What did she need them to do to put her spirit at rest, to break the hold she had on the house and on Teddy? The answers seemed just out of reach, hidden behind the frost and the fear.

For now, their main priority was Teddy. They needed to keep him safe, to keep him warm, and to keep him alive. As Wesley looked into Charlie's frightened eyes, he knew that they were in this together, bound by a shared determination to protect the child they both loved.

The house seemed to breathe around them, the air thick with anticipation and dread.

As the temperature continued to drop and the windows frosted over with more urgent, fragmented messages, Wesley knew that they were running out of time. They needed to find a way out, to break the hold that Evelyn had on them, to save Teddy before it was too late.

But for now, they were trapped.

* * *

Wesley's mind raced as he took in the chaotic state of the house. The pipes groaned and shuddered, the sound of water freezing within them echoing through the walls. The creaking of the floors and walls took on an ominous tone, as if the very structure of the house was crying out in pain. The air grew colder still, their breaths misting in front of them like miniature clouds.

He looked at Charlie, who held Teddy close, trying to

share his warmth with his son. The fear in Charlie's eyes reflected his own. They were still trapped, and the house was turning against them, or rather, Evelyn's grief and rage were manifesting in ways that threatened their safety.

"We need to find that manuscript," Wesley said, his voice steady despite the turmoil inside him. "It's not just about preserving history anymore. It might be the key to helping Evelyn find peace."

Charlie nodded, understanding dawning in his eyes. "The lullaby was her connection to Alaric. But what if there's more? What if she wrote something after, something that could help her... move on?"

Wesley agreed, his thoughts aligning with Charlie's. "Exactly. She couldn't say it in words, but maybe she encoded it in her music. We need to find out what that is."

The sound of cracking ice echoed through the empty rooms, sending a shiver down Wesley's spine. Evelyn's desire to protect Teddy was becoming destructive, and they were caught in the middle of it.

The music room materialized around them, but not as the ghostly apparition they'd seen before. This time it felt solid, real; a space that had existed all along, hidden behind decades of remodeling and forgotten memories.

"Look," Charlie whispered, pointing to the grand piano against the far wall. Unlike the spectral instrument they'd witnessed before, this one was physical, its wood dulled with age but still elegant.

Wesley approached carefully, his trained eye noting details that placed the piano's age: the particular style of carved legs, the slightly yellowed ivory keys, the distinctive maker's mark that had stopped being used after 1892. This wasn't a manifestation of Evelyn's memories; this was her actual piano.

Behind it, tucked almost invisibly against the wall, sat a leather-bound volume.

"That's it," Wesley breathed, recognizing the type of binding commonly used for personal journals and music collections in the late Victorian era. "That's what she wants us to find."

The house creaked around them, the sound almost approving. But as Wesley reached for the journal, the temperature plummeted again. Not in anger this way, but in memory. It was as if the house itself was preparing them for what they were about to learn.

* * *

The journal's leather binding was stiff with age, but Wesley handled it with the careful reverence he'd learned during his years of archival research. Each page might hold not just music, but answers; the truth behind what had happened that winter day in 1895.

Charlie hovered nearby, still holding Teddy close. "What is it?" he asked, his voice hushed as if he too could feel the weight of history in the room.

"It's her personal manuscript book," Wesley explained, recognizing the common practice of the era. "Musicians, especially well-educated young women like Evelyn, would use these to compose and collect their pieces. But look-" he pointed to certain pages where musical notation gave way to hurried writing. "She used it as a diary too.

Probably her only private space to record what was really happening."

"There's something else," Charlie said suddenly, pointing to a detail Wesley had missed. Small water stains dotted the pages, but they weren't random damage. They formed a pattern, like... "Teardrops," Charlie whispered. "She was crying when she wrote this."

The house groaned, a sound like ice breaking over deep water. Above them, they could hear the distinctive notes of a piano key being struck: middle C, then E flat, then G. A minor chord that made both men shiver.

The house's temperature continued to drop, but now it felt less threatening and more... anticipatory. As if the building itself was holding its breath, waiting for them to understand.

"She's trying to tell us something else," Wesley said, trying to make sense of the pattern. "The music, the tears, the ice..."

The minor chord hung in the air for a moment before the room itself began to shift around them. Wesley clutched the manuscript closer, his instincts screaming to protect the document even as the supernatural chaos erupted. They had to go. Now.

They moved quickly, Wesley clutching the manuscript in a vice grip as they navigated the increasingly chaotic house. The music room appeared and disappeared at random as they filed through the doorway, the grand piano playing a haunting melody one moment and vanishing the next. Doors opened to impossible spaces, revealing glimpses of the past: a laughter-filled parlor, a bustling kitchen, a quiet study, before slamming shut again.

Charlie's grip on Teddy tightened as the boy grew more difficult to wake, his form becoming almost translucent, as if Evelyn's presence was drawing him deeper into the past. "Teddy, stay with me, buddy," Charlie pleaded, his voice choked with fear.

Wesley led them through the house, his mind racing as he tried to make sense of the supernatural phenomena. The manuscript seemed to react to their surroundings, the pages fluttering as if caught in an unseen breeze, the musical notes shifting and rearranging themselves.

As they passed the staircase, the banister transformed into a cascade of ice, the frost spreading rapidly across the floor. Wesley skidded to a halt, pulling Charlie back just as the ice reached their feet. The house was fighting back, Evelyn's grief and rage manifesting in ways that were becoming increasingly dangerous.

"We need to find somewhere safe," Wesley said, his breath misting in the cold air. "Somewhere we can look at the manuscript without being interrupted."

Charlie nodded, his eyes scanning the shifting landscape of the house. "The attic," he suggested. "It's small, and it hasn't changed like the rest of the house."

Wesley agreed, and they made their way to the attic, the house groaning and creaking around them as if trying to impede their progress. The attic was untouched by the chaos below, the air slightly warmer and the space quiet, save for the distant sound of the piano playing its haunting melody.

Charlie laid Teddy down on a pile of blankets, the boy's form barely visible beneath the thick fabric. Wesley sat beside them, the manuscript open on his lap. He could feel the weight of Evelyn's emotions in the pages, the music a tangible link to her past.

As he began to read the notes, the music room appeared before them, the grand piano playing the melody from the manuscript. The room was filled with a sense of longing and sorrow, the air thick with unshed tears. Wesley could feel Evelyn's presence, her spirit drawn to the music, her emotions raw and unfiltered.

Charlie looked at Wesley, his eyes filled with a mix of fear and determination. "We need to help her now," he said, his voice steady despite the turmoil inside him. "We need to help her find peace, or Teddy might..."

Wesley nodded, his fingers tracing the musical notes on the page. The answers were hidden within the music, the truth of Evelyn's past waiting to be uncovered. And as the piano played its haunting melody, Wesley knew that they were close to finding the key to helping Evelyn move on, to breaking the hold she had on the house and on Teddy.

But time was running out, and with each passing moment, Teddy was drawn deeper into the past, his form becoming more translucent, his breaths growing shallower. The house groaned around them, the temperature dropping further, the ice spreading rapidly. They were in a race against time, a battle against the supernatural, and the stakes had never been higher.

Wesley's head snapped up from the journal. "It's in the walls." He stood and began feeling around the aged wallpaper of the attic space, ignoring Charlie's bewildered expression.

* * *

Wesley's fingers trembled as he peeled back the yellowed wallpaper, his touch gentle despite their urgency. Years of archival work had taught him how to handle fragile materials, but nothing in his studies had prepared him for this moment. The house shuddered around them, the air growing colder with each passing second. Charlie stood beside him, clutching Teddy tightly, the boy's form growing increasingly translucent.

The hidden compartment finally revealed itself: a common feature in Victorian homes, Wesley knew, where families often concealed important documents. Inside lay a bundle of papers tied with a faded purple ribbon, the color choice distinctly personal rather than official. His heart raced as he carefully extracted them, recognizing the type of paper commonly used for musical notation in the 1890s.

"This is it," Wesley whispered, his voice barely audible over the groaning of the house. "These are Evelyn's original compositions."

Charlie leaned in, supporting Teddy with one arm while reaching toward the papers with his free hand. "But why hide them here? Why not with her other belongings?"

Wesley's eye caught a detail at the bottom of one page: a hurried notation in different ink, the handwriting more desperate than the careful musical notes above. "Because Robert didn't want anyone to find them," he said, anger coloring his voice. "Look at these water marks, the torn edges. He tried to destroy them, but someone..." Wesley paused, studying the repair work. "Someone saved them. Preserved them."

The house reacted violently to this discovery, the temperature plummeting. Ice crystals formed on the windows in distinct patterns; not random frost, the same decorative designs Wesley had seen in photographs of the estate's original conservatory. The pipes groaned as water froze within them, the sound eerily similar to distant crying.

"Evelyn knew," Wesley said, carefully unfolding a page that had been pressed between two others. "She wasn't just writing music, she was documenting everything. Some Victorian women, especially unmarried ones living under male guardianship, would encode their true thoughts in seemingly innocent activities like music composition or flower pressing." His voice grew stronger as his academic knowledge provided a framework for understanding. "She was leaving evidence."

Charlie's face hardened as he looked at the pages. "Evidence of what Robert did?"

"More than that." Wesley pointed to a series of notations that didn't quite match standard musical annotation. "It looks like she may have developed her own system here: see how these notes don't follow conventional patterns? She was likely writing in code, telling the whole story, knowing Robert wouldn't understand enough about music theory to realize what she was doing."

The floor beneath them creaked, and frost began spreading from the corners of the room. This time, it felt less threatening, more like the house was confirming their discovery, urging them to continue.

Wesley turned another page and found what they'd been seeking: a letter sealed with wax and hidden among the sheet music. His hands shook as he broke the seal, the sound of cracking wax echoing in the frozen air.

The letter's contents would change everything: not only their understanding of what happened that winter day; it could improve their chance of helping both Evelyn and Teddy. As Wesley began to read, the house seemed to hold its breath, ice and memory suspended in perfect, terrible clarity.

* * *

The air in the attic grew dense with an otherworldly energy, like the pressure before a thunderstorm. The manuscript trembled in Wesley's hands, its pages fluttering with a wind that shouldn't exist indoors. Charlie huddled over Teddy, his breath visible in the plummeting temperature, as the familiar walls of the attic began to twist and groan.

Evelyn materialized before them, more corporeal than they'd ever seen her. The fury of her manifestation made the protection mirrors they'd brought from Teddy's room vibrate, their reflective surfaces catching and multiplying her image until it seemed like dozens of Evelyns surrounded them. Her dark hair whipped around her face, and Wesley noticed for the first time how much she resembled the portrait in the letter's seal.

"He lied," she cried, her voice resonating with a power that seemed to shake the foundations of the house. Each word frosted in the air as she spoke. "Robert lied, and Alaric died because of it."

The house responded to her anguish, transforming around them like a terrible blooming flower. The wooden beams dissolved into winter sky, the walls melting away to reveal the expanse of the frozen lake from 1895. The same lake they'd seen in the historical society's photographs, but now horrifyingly real. Ice stretched before them; its surface marked with deliberate cracks.

Not natural formations; the evidence of Robert's calculated negligence.

The air filled with sounds: the distant piano playing Evelyn's lullaby, children's laughter echoing across the ice, and underneath it all, the terrible creaking of weakened ice about to give way. All the sounds they'd been hearing throughout the house, now woven together into its own haunting symphony.

Wesley watched in horror as the lake continued to form around them, trying to catalogue details even as reality warped. The ice that crept up the walls carried the same patterns as the frost messages on the windows downstairs. The spectral light matched the winter afternoon described in Evelyn's coded musical notes. Everything they'd witnessed, every supernatural occurrence in the house, had been building to this moment.

Charlie clutched Teddy tighter, his eyes wide with fear as he looked out at the lake. "Wesley," he managed, his voice barely above a whisper. "What's happening?"

"The house is remembering," Wesley said, understanding dawning as he connected the fragments of evidence they'd gathered. "It's trying to show us the truth. The whole truth: not just what happened on the ice, but why." He gestured to the manuscript in his hands. "Everything Evelyn documented, everything she tried to warn people about; the house is making it real."

Teddy's form flickered like a candle flame, becoming more translucent as Evelyn's presence intensified. His eyes fluttered open, and for a moment, Wesley saw Alaric's face superimposed over Teddy's; not just similar as they'd thought before, a perfect match, down to the small scar above his left eyebrow that Evelyn had noted in her writings.

The ice continued to spread, claiming the space inch by frozen inch. The air grew so cold it hurt to breathe, each inhalation carrying the sharp bite of that fatal winter day. Evelyn stood at the edge of the forming lake, her gaze fixed on a distant figure barely visible through the swirling snow: a small boy, drawn by the glint of something metal on the ice.

"Alaric," she whispered, the name carrying all the weight of her century-old grief. The ice beneath her feet cracked with a sound like a gunshot, but she didn't flinch. She'd heard this sound before, had relived this moment countless times.

Wesley could feel the danger building, the house responding to Evelyn's surging emotions. It was a convergence of past and present, memory and reality, truth and consequence. The manuscript in his hands grew colder, its pages turning by themselves to reveal the final measures of Evelyn's last composition: not a lullaby, a requiem.

They were running out of time.

* * *

Wesley's breath frosted in the air as he stared at the spectral scene unfolding before them, his mind racing to connect every piece they'd discovered. The mysterious writing in the kitchen cabinets, the vanishing cereal, Teddy's strange exhaustion, the locked doors. It hadn't been random haunting activity. Every manifestation had been Evelyn trying to protect Teddy, trying to prevent history from repeating itself. That they already knew.

"We can't just stand here," Charlie whispered, his voice

raw with the same protective determination that had led him to fill Teddy's room with mirrors and herbs. "We have to help her let go."

Wesley nodded, thinking back to how the house had responded to their earlier attempts at communication. The salt lines that had actually seemed to help, the mirrors that had caught glimpses of the past.

He took a deep breath, tasting ice and memory on his tongue. "Evelyn," he called out, his voice steady despite the supernatural chaos around them. "We found your manuscript. We know what happened, not just about Alaric. About Robert. About the ice."

The figure on the lake turned, her dark hair whipping around her like a mourning veil. Her eyes were wide with anguish, but there was something else there now, recognition, awareness. The same look she'd worn in that last photograph, the one taken just days before the tragedy.

"I failed," she whispered, her voice carrying the weight of a century's grief. "I knew the ice was weak. I saw Robert testing it the night before, saw him marking the spots that wouldn't hold. But I thought... I thought keeping them close to shore would be enough."

Charlie's grip on Teddy tightened, but not from fear this time. "That's why you've been trying so hard to protect Teddy," he said softly. "You saw the warning signs back then but couldn't stop it. You're trying to make sure no one else misses them."

The house groaned around them, ice crackling up the walls. But the sound was different now, less threatening and more... mournful. Like the house itself was acknowledging the truth.

Wesley stepped forward, the manuscript cold in his hands. "You didn't fail, Evelyn," he said, drawing on everything they'd learned. "Your music, your coded messages. They preserved the truth. You made sure Robert's crime wouldn't stay buried, even if it took a century for someone to understand."

"But Alaric-" her form flickered, grief threatening to overwhelm her again.

"You tried to save him," Charlie interrupted, his voice gentle but firm. "You gave your life trying to protect him. That's not failure, Evelyn. That's love."

Teddy stirred in Charlie's arms, his eyes opening. For a moment, the boy they knew shone through clearly, separate from any echo of Alaric. "The pretty lady's crying," he said softly, reaching toward Evelyn with one small hand.

The gesture, so innocent and pure, seemed to break something in the atmosphere. The ice stopped spreading, the terrible cold holding steady instead of deepening. Evelyn's form stabilized, her expression shifting from anguish to something more complex.

"I don't know how to let go," she whispered, echoing her words from earlier. But this time, they weren't just words of grief. They were a request for help.

Wesley looked down at the manuscript, then at Charlie. They both knew what needed to happen next. Just as Evelyn had used music to preserve the truth, they would need to use it to help her find peace. But first, she had to understand that protecting Teddy didn't mean trapping him in the past.

"You can protect him without controlling him," Charlie

said, taking a careful step forward. "I do it every day. It's terrifying, letting him take risks, letting him grow. But that's what love is: being there to catch them when you can and being strong enough to let them find their own way."

The house shuddered around them; this time it felt like acceptance rather than resistance. The ice beneath their feet remained solid, no longer cracking with the weight of memory and guilt.

Evelyn looked at Teddy, then at Charlie, her expression softening with dawning understanding. The piano music that had haunted the house changed subtly, the mournful requiem giving way to something gentler; not quite a lullaby, instead it was a melody of acceptance and letting go.

* * *

The frozen lake stretched endlessly around them, though something had changed in its appearance. The ice no longer seemed threatening; instead, it held a crystalline beauty, like a moment preserved in glass. Wesley could feel the manuscript's weight in his hands, the physical pages held the weight of a century's worth of unspoken truth.

Charlie cradled Teddy, who had grown more solid again, no longer flickering between past and present. The boy watched Evelyn with clear eyes, fully himself yet somehow bridging the gap between then and now. "The music's different," he said softly. "It's not sad anymore."

He was right. The ghostly piano notes that had haunted the house had transformed, weaving together fragments they'd heard before: the lullaby Evelyn wrote for Alaric, the requiem hidden in her final composition, and something new, something that spoke of acceptance rather than grief.

"The manuscript," Wesley said suddenly. "It's your legacy, Evelyn. Everything you were: teacher, protector, musician; they're preserved in these pages."

Evelyn's form solidified further as she turned toward the piano that had materialized on the ice. Her fingers hovered over the keys, not quite touching. "I wrote so many pieces," she said, her voice steadier now. "Happy ones, when the boys were learning to dance. Quiet ones, for stormy nights when they couldn't sleep. And the last one..." She looked at Charlie. "The one I wrote when I knew what Robert had done, when I knew I had to protect them somehow."

"Play it," Charlie said quietly. "Not the grief this time. Play what you want them to remember."

Evelyn's hands descended onto the keys, and music filled the air; it replaced the haunting melodies of before with something rich with memory and love. As she played, the ice beneath their feet began to transform, becoming transparent enough to see what lay beneath: not darkness and death, but preserved moments of joy. Children skating, Evelyn teaching Alaric his scales, Joseph's first stumbling waltz.

Wesley watched in awe as the house responded, its structure settling around them like a sigh. The temperature began to rise, not suddenly but gradually, like winter giving way to spring. He could feel the change in the manuscript too, the pages warming under his fingers as if finally ready to share their full story.

"I remember now," Teddy said, but his voice was entirely his own. "Not like before. But I can see it, like pictures in a book. You loved them so much."

Evelyn's music swelled, and with it came a lightness, a lifting of the heavy atmosphere that had permeated the house. The truth was out: about Robert's betrayal, about Alaric's fate, about Evelyn's sacrifice. More importantly, the love that had driven everything that had preserved these memories for over a century was finally free to exist without the weight of guilt and grief.

The piano's final notes hung in the air like stars.

*   *   *

As the last note faded, the frozen lake began to recede, not violently but gently, like tide going out. The house's structure reformed around them, with a change; it was now lighter, warmer, as if it too had been freed from a great weight. The music room they found themselves in had solidified into permanent existence, no longer a manifestation of grief but a real space; preserved as Evelyn had known it.

Evelyn's form remained visible. The desperate, frightening energy that had filled the house was gone, replaced by a presence that felt more like warmth than cold, more like protection than possession. She looked at Teddy with clear eyes, seeing him fully as himself now, not as an echo of the past.

"I understand now," she said softly. "Protecting isn't the same as preserving. Living children need to grow, to change." She smiled at Charlie. "To be loved enough to be let go."

The manuscript in Wesley's hands had grown warm, its pages no longer brittle with age but supple, ready to share their stories. The truth about Robert would be known, not only as a source of pain but as a testament to Evelyn's courage. Her music would live on, as more than just as evidence; as the gift she had always meant it to be.

Teddy stirred in Charlie's arms, fully awake now. "Will you still play sometimes?" he asked Evelyn. "Not the sad songs, but the happy ones?"

"When the house remembers joy," she promised, "you'll hear the music."

The morning light began to filter through the windows; real windows now, no longer frosted with desperate messages. The temperature settled into natural warmth, and the doors quietly unlocked themselves.

Wesley looked at Charlie and Teddy, at the manuscript that would tell Evelyn's story, at the music room that would remain as a reminder of love that transcended tragedy. The supernatural hadn't ended, they could all feel that; it had become something that enhanced life rather than trapped it.

The house creaked gently, a sound that no longer carried warning but welcome. Evelyn's form began to fade in peace, her presence settling into the house's bones like music written into memory.

They had found more than truth in the Hawthorne Estate. They had found healing, for both the living and the dead. And as the morning sun painted the music room in shades of gold, they could hear, very faintly, the sound of a piano playing a lullaby, to remind them that even the deepest winters eventually yield to spring.

EPILOGUE

Morning sunlight streamed through the kitchen windows, casting warm patches on the hardwood floor. The frost was gone, leaving the glass clear and bright, and the house hummed with a peaceful energy that felt nothing like the desperate cold of the day before. Teddy sat at the table, happily munching his way through a bowl of cereal while telling elaborate stories about his stuffed lion's adventures.

Wesley watched the boy carefully, exchanging subtle glances with Charlie. There was no trace of trauma in Teddy's bright eyes, no hint that he remembered anything unusual about their visit. When he spoke of the house, it was with simple childish enthusiasm about the big rooms and interesting shadows, not about invisible friends or mysterious music.

"Can I help unpack more boxes?" Teddy asked between bites. "I'm really good at finding stuff!"

Charlie ruffled his son's hair, relief evident in his smile. "Sure, buddy. But no climbing on furniture, okay?"

While Teddy was distracted by a particularly challenging spoonful of cereal, Charlie leaned closer to Wesley. "He doesn't remember any of it," he whispered. "Not Evelyn, not the ice, nothing."

"Maybe that's for the best," Wesley replied softly. The trauma of their experience still felt raw but watching Teddy's innocent enjoyment of his breakfast made it easier to bear.

A faint melody drifted through the air, just a few notes, gentle and sweet. Wesley and Charlie tensed automatically, but Teddy just smiled. "The house makes pretty music sometimes," he said matter-of-factly, as if commenting on the weather. "Like a big music box."

The adults shared another look, this one filled with understanding. It seemed like Evelyn was still there, but her presence had transformed from desperate haunting to gentle guardianship. The house remembered, even if Teddy didn't.

* * *

They spent the late morning tackling the boxes that had been abandoned during the supernatural events. Wesley found himself automatically cataloging each item's historical significance as he unpacked with a deeper appreciation for the stories objects could tell.

"Look what I found!" Teddy's voice rang out from the hallway. Charlie and Wesley hurried over to find him holding a small cloth bag of dried herbs, one of the many protective measures they'd desperately employed just days ago.

Charlie laughed, though the sound held a touch of remembered fear. "My great spiritual protection shopping spree," he said, shaking his head. "Man, I can't believe I bought so much sage."

"At least it made the house smell nice," Wesley offered, remembering their near-hysterical attempts to cleanse the space. "Very... herbaceous."

They continued unpacking, falling into an easy rhythm. During moments when Teddy was occupied with arranging his toys in his room, the adults spoke quietly about their shared experience.

"I found a therapist," Charlie said, carefully wrapping a photo frame in bubble wrap. "Someone who specializes in trauma. I figured we both might need... you know."

Wesley nodded, thinking of how to explain their experience without mentioning supernatural elements. "I've got a recommendation too. Different practice, though. Probably better that way."

"How do we even begin to talk about it?" Charlie wondered, his hands stilling on the box he was unpacking.

"We tell the truth," Wesley said after a moment. "Just... maybe not all of it. The important parts are real enough: facing our fears, protecting what matters, learning to let go."

They worked their way through the house, organizing and arranging. Wesley's study took special care, with Evelyn's manuscript and his research about the house taking pride of place on a shelf near his desk. The music room, no longer appearing and disappearing at will, had become a normal part of the house's layout, though it still held an undeniable energy that made both men pause whenever they passed its open door.

Teddy's voice drifted down from upstairs, humming a tune that made them both stop and listen. It was Evelyn's lullaby, though the boy had no memory of learning it.

* * *

The last rays of sunset painted the living room in warm golds and soft purples as Charlie folded another shirt, adding it to his nearly-packed suitcase. Wesley sat in the armchair nearby, laptop open as he reviewed details for his upcoming first day at the university's history department.

"You'll call when you get home?" Wesley asked, trying to keep his voice casual despite the slight anxiety that crept in. After everything they'd been through, the idea of Charlie and Teddy leaving felt stranger than it should.

"Of course," Charlie smiled, understanding in his eyes. "And we'll be back in a few weeks. Can't let you forget what it's like having a four-year-old tornado around."

"Three weeks," Teddy corrected from his spot on the floor, where he was conducting an elaborate rescue mission with his stuffed animals. "Daddy promised."

The adults shared a smile, watching Teddy play. He hummed softly as he moved his toys around: that same familiar melody they'd heard so often now, though he had no conscious memory of its source. The house seemed to hum with him, its settled sounds harmonizing in a way that no longer frightened them.

"I made us both appointments," Charlie said quietly,

folding another shirt. "Different days, different counselors like you suggested. Dr. Mitchell for me, Dr. Lewis for you. They're supposed to be good with... unusual trauma."

Wesley nodded, closing his laptop. "Good. We should probably..." he glanced at Teddy, lowering his voice further, "probably work through some of this before it becomes something bigger."

"Yeah," Charlie agreed. "Though I still have no idea how to explain why I bought every protective herb in the state."

Their soft laughter was interrupted by Teddy's gentle snoring. They looked over to find him curled up on the rug, his lion clutched close, face peaceful in sleep. As Charlie moved to pick him up, a faint piano melody drifted through the house - not the desperate notes they'd heard during the haunting, but something softer, almost like a benediction.

Charlie and Wesley exchanged glances, but neither felt any fear. The music was part of the house now, as natural as creaking floorboards or settling foundations. A reminder, not a warning.

* * *

Morning dew sparkled on the lawn as Charlie loaded the last bag into his car. Teddy bounced excitedly on the porch steps, already talking about what they'd do on their next visit. Wesley leaned against the porch railing, trying to memorize this moment; the normalcy of it, the peace.

"You'll text when you get home?" he asked again, earning a playful eye roll from Charlie.

"Yes, mom," Charlie teased, then grew serious. "Take care of yourself, man. And..." he glanced at the house, "take care of her too."

"I will," Wesley promised, understanding all Charlie meant. He crouched down to Teddy's level. "And you, mister, be good for your dad."

"I will!" Teddy hugged him tight. "Can we play blocks again when we come back?"

"Absolutely."

Wesley stood on the porch long after their car had disappeared down the street, the morning sun warming his shoulders. The weight of everything that had happened settled around him like a familiar coat; heavy at times, but no longer crushing.

Inside, he walked to the music room, now as much a part of his home as his study or kitchen. The piano stood silent but well-tended, its wood gleaming in the morning light. He wasn't imagining the warmth in the air, or the feeling of peaceful watchfulness that permeated the space.

"I'll take good care of it," he said softly, running a hand along the piano's polished surface. "All of it."

As if in response, a few gentle notes sounded; not from the physical piano, instead from somewhere just beyond normal hearing. The song of something that remembered joy as well as sorrow, of a guardian who had learned to protect without possessing.

Wesley smiled and headed to his study. He had documents to prepare, a manuscript to preserve, and a home to fully settle into. The Hawthorne Estate had more stories to tell, but now they were stories of healing rather than haunting, of memory rather than mourning.

As he closed his study door, the house settled around him with a sound like a contented sigh. Somewhere upstairs, a piano played a few more quiet notes of welcome, no longer a lament for what was lost.

Life, Wesley realized, would never be quite normal again. But maybe it would be something better, something that acknowledged both the rational and the mysterious, the historical and the supernatural, the past and the present. Something that remembered love in all its forms, even across the boundaries of time itself.

ABOUT THE AUTHOR

Jay D. Falor's fiction emerges from a life spent exploring Earth's most evocative places. From summoning ceremonies in Scottish Highlands to nights spent in Roman nunneries, they've gathered tales where magic seems possible. Their studies of ancient cultures, from Mayan ruins to London's historic towers, inform the complex societies in their works. Born in Louisiana and raised in Sydney, their agender perspective brings fresh insight to questions of identity and belonging in speculative fiction. Their worlds challenge readers to imagine possibilities beyond traditional boundaries, whether exploring distant planets or the depths of human experience.

In the Halls of the Haunted

www.ingramcontent.com/pod-product-compliance
Lightning Source LLC
Chambersburg PA
CBHW010612310726
48969CB00010B/2667